The Trouble with Paradise

I0592879

ANNIE SEATON

Richards Brothers: Book 1

Originally published as Holiday Affair, March 2012
Copyright © 2012 by Annie Seaton, revised and expanded May 2019.

To Ian, my wonderful husband of many years...you are *always* there for me.

Chapter One

Melissa McIntyre sat on the side of the timber sailing ship as it rounded the point into Butterfly Bay on the north side of Hook Island in the Whitsunday Islands. Reaching down for her camera, Lissy smiled as she caught her reflection in the smoky black glass of the hatch window beside her. Emerald green eyes surrounded by a tangle of sun-streaked auburn curls twinkled back at her. The days spent basking in the warmth around the pool at Hamilton Island over the last week had deepened her tan and she had almost forgotten it was winter back home on the New England tablelands.

"No more prim and proper Dr McIntyre." She smiled to herself. Looking down at her raggedy denim shorts and the bare tanned feet resting on her rucksack, she grinned as she imagined the reaction of her history colleagues at the university if they could see the elegant Dr McIntyre in backpacker mode.

Strands of hair were pushed across her face

by the breeze, and she lifted her hand to brush them away; she didn't want to miss one second of this amazing view.

Sails snapped sharply as the wind caught them and the crew scurried to tighten the ropes, calling to each other as they worked to bring the sails down as the beautiful old timber schooner eased into the bay for its overnight anchorage.

The musical tone of backpackers chatting in different languages provided a cheerful end to the first day of her sailing adventure. The vessel was crowded with young people from many countries, and everywhere she looked they seemed to be in couples. An unfamiliar pang of loneliness tried to settle in her chest, but she pushed it away.

Lifting her camera, Melissa stood and positioned herself to capture the best view of the sunset. When she went back to work, she'd put the photo on her computer desktop and remember this beautiful place when the winter weather got her down.

She blinked as a rugged face filled the viewfinder, blocking her view of the sky, and one brilliant blue eye winked as a member of the crew peered cheekily into her camera from afar. She leaned back and took a quick distant shot of the guy up the mast, and then turned to snap a series of images of the sun setting over the water as flashes of pink, silver-tipped clouds suffused the sky, and the golden orb slipped towards the horizon. Lowering the camera, she waited as the sailor climbed down the mast towards her. He swung down on the lower ropes, his deep voice serenading her with a bawdy sea shanty. She laughed and finished off the last two lines of the song with him.

"What shall we do with a drunken sailor? Put him in bed with the captain's daughter?" He stopped beside the deck esky and held up a can of beer and a small bottle of wine.

"Wine or beer?"

"Wine, please," she said with a shy smile. She'd barely spoken to anyone all day; just the usual greetings as the passengers boarded the boat and found their own place to sit. Melissa liked her own company and had been happy keeping to herself. The sailor closed the lid of the esky and sat on the step beside her.

"Cheers. I'm Nick." He handed her a small plastic wine cup and she waited while he unscrewed the bottle, and then poured it in. He put the empty wine bottle in the bin beside them and lifted the plastic water bottle as he tilted his head to the side with a questioning look. "A toast to the sunset?"

She nodded and smiled at him as she lifted her glass. "Just water for you?' she asked.

"Yes, I'm on duty for another hour, but then the fun begins," he said and flashed her a cheeky smile. "But now, a toast to a beautiful lady."

Melissa caught her breath as deep blue eyes locked with hers. Her hand shook as he captured her fingers and she squeezed the plastic cup with her other hand. He was almost too good-looking. A bright blue bandana held back a thatch of shaggy sun-bleached hair. She held his gaze as he touched his water bottle against her wine. Dr. McIntyre would have blushed, but Melissa McIntyre took it in her stride. It wasn't every day that a man as gorgeous as he was, sang to you and offered you a toast. She took it in the holiday spirit, which she was sure he'd intended, although he did hold her gaze a little longer than a casual look called for.

"Thanks, and cheers. I'm Lissy."

"Backpacking?" He sat comfortably next to her, his muscled legs stretched out on the timber deck, his shoulder resting casually against hers.

She looked up at him and felt a strange unfamiliar urge to pull loose the bandana and run her fingers through his shaggy hair.

Where on earth had that come from?

"Sort of," she finally replied, and her voice was husky.

Nick turned to her, revealing laugh lines around his deep blue eyes and sexy mouth. He was a fair bit older than she had first thought.

"Just a bit of a trip around North Queensland. How about you?" She was not going to give away too much. She wasn't ready yet to slip back into her real world of boring history professor. She had found comfort in being her Gramps's *Lissy* in the ten days since she'd scattered his ashes on Blackrock Beach and then flown to the tropics for a restful holiday.

"Same. Just crewing on the boat for a friend for a few weeks," he replied. "Speaking of which, I'd better go and help with the anchor. We're almost to the island." He tipped his head back, swigging the rest of his water. He grasped the rope to swing himself to the upper deck, the muscles in his arms bunching. Giving her a broad wink, he grinned cheekily at her.

"Save a dance for me tonight, Angel Face." Nick headed to the bow of the vessel with a swagger that would have done a pirate proud, chatting and joking with the other passengers as he went. It was almost a primitive sexuality that surrounded him, dangerous to any woman. He was one of the best-looking men she had ever seen, and an unfamiliar warmth ran through her. Reluctantly, she dragged her eyes away from the breadth of his tanned back and tautly muscled legs as a voice interrupted her thoughts.

"Half your luck. You've been chosen for the night."

Lissy turned to see a blonde girl in the charter company's uniform looking at her with a bemused expression. "Excuse me?"

"You're obviously the chosen one for tonight."

Unease unfurled in her chest. "What do you mean?"

"Nick had the same bet with the crew last trip. He picks his conquest for the party on the way into the bay. The woman he chooses to share a drink with before we moor, is the chosen one, and the crew bet on it either way, depending on their impression of the girl. I overheard the boys laughing about it last trip."

Lissy cursed herself for her naiveté.

"Thanks for the warning, but they'll lose their money. I'm not interested."

"Your call, but he is a good catch if you can pin him down." The girl shrugged as she gathered up the empty cups and made her way towards the galley. "No one has been able to, so far."

Lissy mouthed a very rude word under her breath.

The hide and confidence of the man, how dare he think she looked like an easy target?

No matter how good looking he is.

Then again, look at yourself, Lissy McIntyre. Swigging wine on a backpacker's yacht in tattered shorts and with tangled hair, is not a look the usually staid Dr. Melissa McIntyre, of the elegant French roll and navy-blue suits, should be comfortable with.

Melissa gritted her teeth, curling her fists by her sides.

Even so, it didn't matter how she looked—did he really think she was that easy? History was not going to repeat itself. One absent backpacker father was quite enough for this family.

This guy needs to be taught a lesson.

Her throat ached. Unshed tears stung her eyes as the emotion of the last week caught up with her. The cancellation of her mother's flight from Denmark had left her alone at the memorial service, except for Gramps's fishing mates. As she had looked across the water to the rising sun, she'd whispered the words Gramps had penned for her to read while scattering his ashes to the chilly easterly wind.

"Let the ocean soothe your sorrow. I am now with you always; in the sea, the sands, and the wind." She breathed in deeply as she looked out at the sapphire blue of the Pacific Ocean, letting the serene blue of the water soothe her grief.

The anchor clattered to the sandy bottom of the bay, interrupting her sad thoughts. Brushing the tears away with the back of her hand, she waited for an opportunity to make her move. It wasn't long before Nick turned and walked back towards her, and she caught his eye, blowing him a kiss.

He smiled wickedly at her. "Looking forward to that dance." She watched him swagger to the side of the boat to lower the dinghy, with more than a touch of arrogance in his bearing.

"Me too." She smiled as she stood and bent over in front of him to pick up her rucksack, making sure he got a good view of her legs. Out of the corner of her eye, she watched as two crewmembers gave each other a high five. The anger built in her chest and she gritted her teeth as they helped Nick with the ropes holding the rubber dinghy high on the side of the yacht, joking and laughing.

Picking up her rucksack, she made her way to the group waiting to climb down the rope ladder to the dinghy for the short trip across to the island. Standing next to two Italian girls, she grimaced. They whispered and giggled, pointing at Nick expertly steering the dinghy through the coral heads in the bay. He dropped the first group on the island and turned back to those waiting on the boat. He stood aft, one hand on the tiller, the other shading his eyes from the setting sun, his muscled legs braced against the small waves hitting the boat. Nick looked up to catch her eye, and a slow, sexy grin spread over his face.

She swallowed.

No man had the right to be so sexy.

Melissa was the last to climb down the rope ladder and as she prepared to step across to the dinghy; a rogue wave pushed it away from the side of the old schooner.

"Quick, jump!" yelled Nick. She threw her rucksack into the dinghy and jumped, landing awkwardly on her backside.

"Are you hurt?" Nick put out his hand to help pull her up, his eyes full of concern.

"Only my pride," she said. He took her hand and a tingle of warmth shot up her arm. Her fingers felt weak in his grasp and she fought the urge to snatch her hand away as he looked down at her sprawled half on the floor, and across the seat at the side of the dinghy.

The Italian girls giggled, clapping their hands with delight and pretending to swoon as Nick pulled her up into his arms. He held her firmly against him, the hair-roughened warmth of his chest brushing against her bare shoulders.

"Thank you, she said breathlessly, as she fought the mirth building in her chest.

"No injuries from the fall?" he asked softly. Melissa shook her head and removed her hand from his grip. She sat down on the soft side of the dinghy and Nick steered through the coral to the island where the rest of the crew were setting up camp.

Two hours later, Lissy sat watching the sparks that whirled in the breeze as Nick added more driftwood to the fire. The crew had given them a feast of fresh fish, salad, and tropical fruits. Replete, both tourists and crew settled on sand still warm from the sun. The campfire provided a soft flickering light and one of the backpackers gently strummed his guitar. Melissa gazed into the fire, remembering the days at Blackrock Beach when she and Gramps had fried fresh fish over a driftwood fire on the beach. For the first time in a week, she moved past the grief and found joy in the memory.

"He must have been good." Goose bumps raised on her arms as she felt the warmth of Nick's breath on her neck.

She moved away slightly. "Excuse me?"

"There's only one thing that will put that look on a woman's face," he whispered in her ear.

"Oh yes, he was." She grabbed her rucksack and used it as a pillow. She looked up at the brilliant stars dotting the black sky. "The very best." Gramps had been the only stability she had ever known. If Nick thought she was talking about a previous lover, so be it, since he deserved everything he was about to get.

He held her eyes and then dropped his gaze to linger on her body stretched on the sand. She held her breath as he slowly looked down from her shoulders to her breasts and then back up to capture her gaze. Lissy shivered, imagining the tips of his fingers caressing her skin. The music increased in tempo, and a couple of the girls began to dance on the beach. He leaned down to her, his breath tickling her neck as he whispered in her ear.

"Come on. Dance with me?" She shivered

again, and goose bumps ran down her arm despite the warmth of his body pressing into her side.

He pulled her up and Lissy's eyes held his as he held her close. Wrapping her arms around his neck, she moulded herself to the hard planes of his body and they moved in time with the slow music. Their bare feet slipped through the soft white sand as they danced slowly around the fire, the crackling of the flames and muted guitar music surrounding them. He gently pushed towards her and her lips found their way to his neck, her mouth opening slightly as she inhaled, his musky scent teasing her nostrils.

Closing her eyes, she sighed softly. His hard chest pressed against the softness of her breasts, and she forgot why she was dancing so closely with a stranger. She pretended Nick was someone who cared about her. As he guided her around the fire in time to the soft music, his hand caressed her back. The pressure of his hand increased as he guided them towards the shadows at the edge of the clearing. The first fluttering of panic began in her chest. With every step she became more aware of the proximity and warmth of his body and the temptation she faced. He dropped his lips to her neck and gently sucked on her skin. An explosion of feeling raced from her neck to her stomach. She pulled back gently and looked up at him, giving herself some space between them. She breathed rapidly, her lips slightly parted as Nick looked down at her.

"I admire a woman who knows what she wants." His voice hinted at all sorts of pleasures.

"Mmm … very tempting." She regretted the words as soon as they were out of her mouth.

Get yourself out of this before it's too late.

Standing on her toes, she moved her hands from his neck to his shoulders and put her face close to his.

"What a shame all the tents are so close," she breathed into his ear. "No privacy here, and I do show my 'appreciation' rather loudly."

She pursed her lips, fighting to keep a straight face. She tried to hold back her laughter, imagining herself as a femme fatale, a passionate woman of the world, and a lusty participant in the bedroom. Nothing could be further from the truth— especially the last few years when she'd buried herself in her studies and research.

She quickly lowered her head to hide the laughter in her eyes and Nick pulled her close, whispering in her ear.

"It's okay, babe. I'll take care of you." She looked up at him, tears of laughter threatening to spill over. She swallowed the giggle bubbling in her throat and it came out in a snort. He looked at her with a slight frown, and she reached up as though she was going to kiss him.

"Sorry, mate, you've lost your bet tonight." Pushing him away, Melissa strolled across to the group around the fire and sat down next to the Italian girls. After tying her sarong tightly around her breasts, she clenched her hands to still the shaking of her fingers.

Yeah, a real femme fatale.

Chapter Two

Nick had first noticed her standing apart from the group of noisy backpackers at the marina that morning. Boarding the vessel alone, she had kept to herself all day. Deep in thought as the old schooner sailed across the Whitsunday Passage to Hook Island, he'd noticed her brush away tears a couple of times. He had also taken several long appreciative looks at her sunbathing on the front deck from his vantage point high up the mast as he rigged the sails. After watching her all day, he was not surprised to feel that jolt of heat run through his body when he'd caught her as she'd fallen. She had a tilted nose with a light sprinkling of freckles and full red lips. Red-gold hair fell in a tangle of curls to brush her delicate bare shoulders. She was older than most of the backpackers on the charter but had a maturity and a beauty that made him look again…and again. It would have been an enjoyable way to end his last trip on the boat.

No commitment, no strings attached; just the way he liked it.

Now, Nick was angry at his stupidity in getting himself entangled in this situation on his last day on the boat. It was because of that stupid bet. He'd lost control of the situation because he was so attracted to Lissy. On the other trips this week, he'd simply shared a few flirtatious kisses with the chosen girls to win the bet with the crew. It had been a stupid thing to do, and he wasn't proud of himself.

When he'd looked down at Lissy, he had been lost in her sad, dark eyes. As he shifted his eyes to her soft mouth, her lips had beckoned him. He had only to dip his head slightly and he could have covered her mouth with his own, savouring the tempting sweetness of those luscious lips.

He shook his head in frustration.

What the hell is wrong with me? I'm getting soft.

It was time to get back to work and finish the blasted report or the funding would dry up. The recent calls from his family indicated it was time to go home and be the dutiful son and brother for a while. The emails from his mother hinted at upcoming changes in the family, and how much they missed him. The pull of Italian blood was strong. As much as he hated to admit it, he loved his time back in Armidale on the family farm. *La mia famiglia* ... the close bond that held his brothers and sisters together no matter where they were in the world was fostered by their mother.

"Penny for your thoughts?" He jumped as a

hand touched his arm.

The first woman who had really attracted him for a long time stood in front of him, backlit by the flickering firelight. Smarting from the unflattering image of himself as a Lothario who would make money from a demeaning bet, he knew it was time to make amends.

"You really don't want to know what I'm thinking. Boring thoughts about work," he said. He walked over to the camp fridge, grabbed two beers, and held one out to her. "Peace offering?"

After a pause, she reached for the beer. "Why not?"

They sipped their beers in silence as they walked back to the group sitting around the fire. They sat on the soft sand and Lissy looked over at him and spread her hands. "Can you really call this work?"

He laughed and decided it was not the right time to tell her all about himself, now that she seemed to have forgiven him for his crass behaviour. He would give it a while and then admit that there was more to him than just a drifter in the Islands.

##

The whoosh of waves breaking on the crushed coral beach woke Lissy early the next morning. Rolling onto her stomach, she opened the flap of the one-man tent and propped her chin on her hand, enjoying the view of the old sailing ship silhouetted by the rising sun. She saw tanned muscular legs through her tent flap and sighed at the sight of Nick heading for the water, clad only in a pair of black swimming trunks. Closing her tent flap, she rolled on to her back, crossing her arms on her chest. Even though she knew what Nick had been playing at, she still found him incredibly attractive ... and kind. His apology last night had shown there was more to him

After breakfast, the crew packed up the campsite in preparation for the sail back to Hamilton Island. Lissy and some of the other backpackers climbed to the lookout on the peak of the island. As they reached the top of the path, she caught her breath and moved across to the lookout, taking in the beauty of the view down to Hamilton Island. Patches of brilliant white sand edged the blue waters, backed by verdant green hills on each island.

"Are you coming, Lissy?" Bella, one of the Italian girls, called. "We sail at eleven."

"I'll catch up with you." She glanced at her watch. She stood there for a long time after the others started the trek to the beach. This short holiday had helped her cope with her grief after Gramps's funeral, and she was feeling ready to go back to work. Deep in thought, she jumped as a deep voice intruded in the silence.

"It's the best view in the Whitsunday Islands." Nick stood at her shoulder. "Did you know the islands were first recorded by Captain Cook on Whit Sunday in 1770, and that's how they got their name?" He was standing so close to her she could feel the heat coming from his body as he pointed to the islands spread below them like emeralds on the blue water.

"Not far north from here, Cook ran aground and had to repair his ship, the *Endeavour*." His breath on the side of her face sent goose bumps down her neck. Her serenity disappeared instantly; he was trying his luck again.

Well, two can play this game. My mother might have been a sucker for the first good-looking man that came along, but I won't follow in her footsteps.

"How fascinating. I don't know much history at all," she said, settling into her role. Professor Andrews would be horrified to hear those words from his Pacific history lecturer.

"I'm a little bit scared to walk down the track alone. I heard things rustling in the bush before." She widened her eyes, deciding not to bat her eyelashes as that might be a bit of overkill.

"Nothing to be scared of," he replied, holding out his hand to her. She reached out and held it and an instant electricity seemed to ignite between them. Nick put his warm hands on her bare shoulders, pulling her in close. Her heart thudded and her knees trembled.

"I feel safe now," she said breathlessly, even though safe was far from what she felt. She hoped the combination of her demure expression and the huskiness of her voice would have the desired reaction. She kept her eyes lowered as his hand slid down her arm and he lifted her hand to his mouth. He moved his lips gently across her palm.

"Come on, the dinghy's waiting to take the last group back." He kept hold of her hand as he led her down the track through the coastal she-oak trees. When they were on the beach, hundreds of black butterflies fluttered from the bush at the eastern end of the bay.

"Spectacular, isn't it? That's why they call it Butterfly Bay." He looked down at her and reached across to push a strand of hair from her eyes. "Delicate creatures, a lot like you." She pushed his hand away. She was done playing games.

"You're not going to give up, are you, Nick? What's the time frame on the bet? I told you last night. You've done your money. You chose the wrong girl." She picked up her backpack and stalked across to the waiting dinghy.

***

Nick's body suffused with heat. Fighting to keep his temper, he struggled to maintain an impassive expression. Lissy glared at him from the edge of the water. Nick Richards, who rarely backed away from a challenge, was intimidated by this slip of a woman. He had avoided this sort of situation for years, since Olivia had dumped him for a richer prospect. Heartbroken, he had sworn a pretty face would never suck him in again, and he had enjoyed his playboy "love'em and leave'em" lifestyle of the last ten years. This stupid bet hadn't given him the opportunity to lay down his usual ground rules, and one thing he hated was dishonesty. Now, he was having a strong and genuine attraction thrown back in his face. Strolling over to the dinghy, he picked up the last of the camping gear and turned to face Lissy, hurt driving his words.

"You are an extremely beautiful young woman, Lissy. All bets aside, flaunting yourself to all and sundry gives an impression of availability, whether you mean to or not. I believe there is a word for women who tease and don't deliver the goods." As he headed for the dinghy he looked over his shoulder and drawled, "So sweetheart, take care or you may find yourself in trouble one day."

Chapter Three

Lissy strode along the road from the marina at Hamilton Island down to her beachfront cabin still fuming from Nick's parting shot. She sat with the Italian girls on the front deck listening to their chatter and laughing with them as they tried to converse in two languages. When the vessel moored, she bid a cheery farewell to Bella and Anna, disembarking without a backward glance. The only time she had been near Nick was during the morning briefing by the crew, and he'd ignored her—which suited her fine. His stinging comment would not leave her. She regretted the two days on the backpacker charter. She should have saved her money and stayed in the luxury cabin at the resort. She couldn't believe how rude he'd been. Working in an international playground where people are relaxed and receptive to romance had distorted his view of the way normal people behaved. He'd started the whole mess with his demeaning bet.

Unlocking the door to her cabin, she angrily threw her backpack into the corner. She was upset with herself because even after his nasty comment, she was still aware of the attraction between them.

She had encouraged him a little bit more than necessary. Her T-shirt and shorts followed the backpack into the corner, and she pushed open the door to the luxurious marble bathroom.

A long soak in the hot tub with lots of bubbles would wash the salt out of her hair and clear her mind. She planned on dressing up and relaxing with a glass of wine and dinner in the resort restaurant. Lissy would enjoy the last night of her holiday, before the prospect of going back to the cold winter of the tablelands, and being Dr. Melissa McIntyre at work, resurfaced. Standing in front of the mirror, water filling the large spa bath, she touched her lips, imagining Nick's lips on hers. She could dream—she would never see him again and could file him away as a fantasy.

The bath wasn't the total escape she had hoped for. As the fragrant oils soaked into her skin and the steamy heat lathered her face with moisture, Nick drifted in and out of her thoughts. Damn the man for being so sexy! She sank down in the water and closed her eyes, but images of him climbing the mast, his long, tanned legs lightly covered with blond hair, and standing bare-chested as he steered the little dinghy, flicked through her mind in an erotic slideshow.

Sitting up, Lissy pulled the plug, dismayed at the direction of her thoughts. She climbed out of the bath, dried off and wrapped herself in a soft white towelling robe, and stepped onto the sunny deck to dry her hair. She pulled up the chair on the front deck that overlooked the tropical gardens at the back of the resort. The front door of the neighbouring cabin opened and caught her attention. A red-faced cleaning maid hurried down the pathway in front of the cabins, pulling her cleaning trolley along behind her.

"Apologies, *monsieur*, I will send someone down with fresh towels for you immediately. I am so sorry that your room was not ready."

"Not a problem," drawled a familiar voice. "I'll borrow one from my friend next door." Lissy looked over to see the subject of her erotic daydream standing there wearing nothing but a wicked grin and a small towel strategically placed across his hips.

"Got a spare towel, sweetheart?" Glaring at him, she draped her spare towel over the low wall between their decks before storming inside and slamming the door behind her.

She closed her eyes as Nick's laughter drifted through the open window. The sooner she was on a plane home, the better. Cold weather and work, with no Nick to bother her, was quickly becoming very appealing.

***

Nick strolled into the restaurant an hour later and spotted Lissy sitting alone at a table by the window overlooking the bay. Her chin rested in her hand as she gazed out over the water. With a quiet word to the *maitre d'*, he walked over to her table and sat opposite her.

"You know I'm beginning to think you're following me." Lissy turned and glared at him, but he reached over and took her hand, ignoring the instant tug of attraction as he looked into her eyes.

"Hey, I want to apologise for the way I spoke to you this morning. I was way out of line." Nick had regretted his harsh words all day, and when he realised Lissy was staying at the resort, he had decided to seek her out and apologise. Finding himself in the cabin next door to her had been an unexpected bonus.

"Let's pretend we've just met and forget the last two days. Good food, good wine, a great view, and great company. I owe you a drink for lending me a towel anyway."

To his surprise, Lissy didn't react with the sarcasm he expected.

"Why not? I'm going back to reality tomorrow. I may as well indulge the last night."

He tilted his head to one side. "Indulge?"

"Don't get your hopes up, matey. I'm talking food and wine, nothing else." Her face brightened. "Good company will be a bonus. It's past time that we quit playing games. A civilised meal together, a casual conversation, good memories, and we'll go our separate ways tonight." She held out her hand. "Deal?"

Holding her gaze, he reached over and took her hand. "It's a deal."

Over dinner, Nick talked about his trip around the Pacific over the past few years and Lissy laughed at his stories of thrill-seeking adventures. Parasailing, mountain climbing, volcano viewing, and surfing off isolated islands. If he embellished his adventures a little bit, it was purely for the pleasure of seeing her laugh. He sympathised as she told him about moving from Blackrock Beach to the city and growing up with her mother and first stepfather and then going to boarding school.

"Father?" asked Nick.

"Only Gramps," she said sadly. "My father was an Irish backpacker who married Mum but didn't hang around long enough to meet me. Now she's sampling a variety of nationalities in the husband category. Started off with the Irish boyo, moved on to an Aussie, then an American, and now she lives in Denmark with her fourth husband."

"I can understand why you were a little bit aloof from the backpacker crowd, and that stupid bet made it worse."

"I don't see my mother very often, and when Gramps died a couple of weeks ago, she didn't even make the service." Nick reached out for Lissy's hand across the table as her eyes filled with tears.

"Gramps was the rock in my life and so proud of me. I was hoping to have some good news for him about a promotion in a few weeks, but he died suddenly in his sleep."

He rubbed his thumb across the top of her hand and Lissy seemed unaware of it as she stared into the candle flickering in the centre of the table. He couldn't take his eyes off her face as the love for her grandfather shone from her eyes.

"The last time I visited him, he teased me." She looked up at Nick and the determination in her face surprised him. "He asked me about my plans, and I can still see his faded blue eyes crinkling at me. He didn't believe that I'd commit to my career and he always teased me about ending up with three kids, a house with a white picket fence, and a dog named Rex. And, of course, a husband. Gramps was a great believer in love. But nearly thirty years watching Mum search for it taught me that security is far more important. I'm about to achieve a milestone in my career and I'm well on the way to security."

"What do you do?"

"No, no details," she said. "Let's just be ships that pass in the night. What about you? Family?"

"Yes. Lots of brothers and sisters, all settled down in the country, producing the required grandchildren for my parents. I'm the son with the wanderlust." Looking across at her, he raised his wine glass. "Like you, I'll never settle down. I like my freedom too much." He clinked her glass across the table. "To a happy life. I hope you find what you're looking for and it brings you happiness."

Her brilliant green eyes lit up and a sweet smile spread slowly across her beautiful face as she clinked her glass against his. A little bit of sadness lingered in her eyes, making him feel even more of a louse for the way he'd treated her. The candlelight formed an aureole of light around her auburn curls and she looked back at him, her eyes full of trust. Eyes that could suck a man right in. It was time to get out of here.

Now. Before he did something he'd regret.

"Right," he said briskly, reaching for the bill folder. "My treat. Apology for the last two days?"

"Thanks for listening tonight. You've been sweet." Lissy placed her hand on top of his.

They walked along the path to their cabins, the sweet smell of frangipani blooms wafting over them. Looking up at the white flowers, Lissy stumbled on a thick root at the edge of the path. Nick reached across and placed his arm casually around her shoulders to guide her. Reaching around, he grabbed and twirled a long curl around his finger. He looked down at her and warmth filled his chest. His hand cupped her shoulder and then he gently skimmed his fingertips down her bare arm.

She leaned into him with a long, drawn-out sigh and he pulled her close. He sensed her crying silently before he felt the tears through his shirt and he held her as she cried. His gut clenched as he realised his crass behaviour had added to her troubles the past couple of days. "I'm really sorry, for upsetting you so much." She drew back, looking up at him through her tears. He cupped her jaw, lifting her tear-streaked face so that she was looking directly at him.

"Don't be silly, I came up here to have a break after Gramps died. No need for an apology. I played the game too. A couple of wines has made me emotional. I'm sorry."

He took her hand, squeezed it and held it as they walked back towards the cabins.

When they reached her cabin, Lissy unlocked the door and turned to Nick.

"Thank you for paying for dinner."

He leaned down to kiss her cheek and bid her goodnight. She looked deep into his eyes and the grief and loneliness on her face turned to naked longing. A powerful desire rocked through him as she reached up and brushed a light kiss along his lips.

Nick wanted her with an intensity that he'd never felt before. For a moment, he stilled, aware of her closeness, her touch, and the soft breath of her gentle kiss. He held her gaze until his mouth covered hers. She slid her hands under his silk shirt and sighed into his mouth as she caressed his warm, bare skin. With a groan, he deepened the kiss and his mouth roamed her face and throat as his hands tangled in her luxurious hair. She reached behind her back with one hand, opened the door, and pulled him into her cabin. Her body was quivering, and her lips were warm, heat seeping into him, warming a cold place deep within that had been chilled for too long. Struggling against the need to rush and realising that she needed gentleness, he moved her slowly across the room until the back of her legs pressed against the bed.

"Okay?" he murmured against her mouth. She answered by reaching up and pulling his shirt above his head and then moving down to the buttons on his jeans.

God, am I insane? What am I doing?

***

For a brief moment, Lissy's fingers paused in their journey downward. She must be crazy because she didn't want to stop what she'd started. She reached around and splayed her fingers on the bare skin under his shirt, resting her cheek against his broad chest. Both hands were now under his shirt and his bare skin was warm beneath her fingers.

"Lissy?" he asked softly.

"Shh."

"Are you sure?"

In answer, she slid her hands back around to his chest and one hand skimmed over smooth warm skin. Lissy pressed her face against his chest, feeling the beat of his heart against her cheek. "I can't think of a nicer way to end my holiday."

Nick took her hands in his and gathered her into his arms. His fingers played with her long curls as he held her close. For the first time in a long time, she felt safe and happy. But he was right—she needed to be sure about this. Closing her eyes, she came to an easy decision. Despite her doubts, she wanted him. She needed to feel his skin against hers. She wanted him, of that she had no doubt. Reaching up with one hand, she brushed his face with trembling fingers as his eyes glinted in the moonlight.

"Has anyone ever told you how beautiful you are," he said quietly.

Her own need was mirrored in those deep blue eyes. She lifted her face and touched her lips to his. Nick's hold tightened, but she moved away and sat on the side of the bed.

Waiting. Needing. Wanting.

His strong body was silhouetted by the bright moonlight streaming through the window, and Lissy shivered with anticipation as he moved closer. His breath whispered along her neck as he unbuttoned the small pearl buttons on her silk dress.

"Sweet perfection," he murmured against her lips. He lifted his head and smiled at her, the sexy laugh lines crinkling around his eyes. Lissy caught her breath.

"You're really sure about this?" he asked.

"I'm sure." The room darkened as his head lowered to hers, blotting out the moonlight streaming through the window.

Chapter Four

The faint light of dawn helped Nick search for his clothes that were scattered around the room. Lissy murmured in her sleep. He moved to the side of the bed and stood quietly looking down at her. A tangle of red-gold curls spread across the white lace pillowcase and her face was perfectly serene. If he was to catch his flight, he had to hurry, and he was torn between reaching down and kissing those inviting lips one more time or leaving quietly.

Love and leave 'em mate, time to move on.

But his conscience pricked him, and he looked for a pen to leave her a brief note.

What do I say? Thanks for the sex, it was great. Have a good life?

Running his hand through his hair, he glanced down at his watch and realised if he didn't hurry he would miss his flight. He took one last look at the beautiful woman curled in the king-size bed and moved quietly to the door. Locking it behind him, he stepped out into the early morning.

The resort was already waking for the day and gardeners were sweeping fallen blooms from the paths. Nick said a brief good morning to a worker who was trimming the tree between their cabins.

In his own room, he had a quick shower and threw his casual clothes into his backpack, grimacing as he pulled out trousers and a long-sleeved shirt. He was not looking forward to leaving the tropics. Tossing his bag over his shoulder, he let himself out of his room with one last regretful look at Lissy's cabin, half-hoping she would be standing at the door, so he could say good-bye.

Half an hour later, Nick had checked into the airport on Hamilton Island and was waiting for his flight to board. He pulled his mobile from his pocket and dialled, shaking his head in amusement as the cheery voice of his brother answered, even though it was only six a.m.

"Hey, bro," Nick greeted his older brother.

"What's wrong?"

Nick smiled. Tomas was the staid one of the three brothers and he took life very seriously.

"Something must be wrong. One, you never call, and two, it's hours before you usually get up."

"Nothing's wrong. I just called to say I'm thinking about delaying my trip home until Sunday night."

Where the hell did that come from? he

wondered.

"Well, Nick, you can't," said his brother. "There's a big barbeque to welcome you home on Saturday and Mama would have your guts for garters if you didn't show." Tomas sighed down the phone. "There's a woman involved, isn't there."

His big brother knew him well.

Nick laughed bitterly. "Yep, bro. You know me, can't all be perfect like you. Always a woman. Forget it, I'll be there. I can't upset Mama."

"It's been two years this time. The whole family is coming to dinner and Mama has been cooking all week. Don't let her down."

"Okay, I'll see you Saturday. Tell Mama I'm picking my bike up in Brisbane and I'll be there about six."

Tomas cleared his throat. "With a friend."

"A friend, hey? What sort of friend?"

"You'll meet her on the weekend. Be careful on that highway. I'll see you Saturday. *Ciao.*"

"Looking forward to it, bro. *Ciao.*" Nick shook his head. Tomas was organised and lived his life by a strict routine; they couldn't be any more different. Sometimes it was hard to believe they came from the same family and the news that he had met someone was no surprise. Tomas always said he would marry at thirty-five. He only had a few months to go.

Nick grinned and shook his head. It would

be good to be back home.

The call came for his flight to Brisbane, and he picked up his backpack and headed for the gate.

***

Lissy opened her eyes as sunlight streamed in through the graceful foliage of the tree outside her window, tracing a delicate pattern across the white sheets. Stretching luxuriously, she lay on her back, watching the red blooms of the poinciana tree sway in the soft morning breeze. If she was inclined to believe that the night's events had been a fantasy she had conjured up while lying in her bath, the aches and soreness she felt attested to the experience of the night. She remembered the pleasure they had shared; it was the first time she had ever truly let herself go, not hiding behind her cool facade. The whole night took on a dreamy quality and she'd fallen into a deep sleep after Nick had reached over and kissed her a lingering goodnight in the early hours.

She lay there, wondering how she would feel when she saw him this morning. Even though it had been a night of passion, she still had to put it behind her. She would pack her bags ready to catch her flight, have a civilised breakfast with him, and wish him well as he set off on his next adventure.

Pulling her wet hair into a loose roll after a quick shower, she applied light makeup, smiling as she saw the traces of pink marks on her neck, where

Nick's rough stubble had grazed her. Warmth shot through her—she needed to see him this morning to keep her feelings in perspective.

You can do this; you're a mature woman of the world. Enjoy his company over breakfast, kiss him good-bye, and then go catch your plane.

Stepping out on to the veranda, she looked across to see if there was any sign of life from Nick's cabin. There was a flurry of activity as two cleaning maids dumped sheets and towels into the trolley, pulling a vacuum cleaner through the front door. Lissy walked down the path and she realised she didn't even know his last name. A cold feeling settled in the pit of her stomach.

"Has my friend checked out already?" she asked.

"Yes, he was our first checkout this morning. Gone before sun-up."

She paused, fighting the tightness in her throat as tears threatened to fall. "I'll be out in a couple of minutes. I'm heading for the airport myself."

The girl gave her a wave and lifted fresh towels from the trolley. "Thanks. Have a safe trip."

Gathering her suitcase and backpack, Lissy glanced at her watch, trying to ignore the hurt of Nick leaving without so much as a good-bye. She had shed enough tears over the past two weeks. By the end of today, she would be home and this interlude would be behind her. The genes had really kicked in big time. *Mum would be proud of me. Hah!*

It was just as well he had gone. He was probably running, because he thought she would be the clingy type that wouldn't let go. Nothing could be further from the truth.

She took one last lingering look at the bed and the rumpled sheets before locking the door. Walking through the tropical garden to reception, she took care not to trip over the tree root that had led to her downfall last night. She made her way to the main building, the wheels of her suitcase disturbing the quiet of the garden.

A good lesson in life, Lissy. A warning that it's easy to go with the lust of the moment and get let down every time. Never again. Just think of Mum. We have Declan, and Greg, and Lincoln and Lars...and then whoever Mum marries next!

"Okay, look on the bright side," her positive side reminded her. "When I am old and grey in my rocking chair, watching my grandchildren play around my feet, I will look back with fond memories and dream about the kind pirate who stole my heart for one night. A bit like the old lady in Titanic."

"Bollocks," chipped in her negative side. "I have to have children, before the grandchildren come along." She thought back to her last conversation with Gramps. After he had teased her about the white picket fence and the dog named Rex, he had put his gnarled hands on each side of her face.

"Sweetheart, believe in love. It's out there waiting for you."

"Gramps," she argued, "I don't believe in romantic love and happily ever after."

Gramps had always said, "Wait and see, my darling. Love makes a fool of plans. Wait for your destiny and promise me you won't settle for less." He had constantly teased her about her weekly outing with Tom, one of her work colleagues, a quiet friend for whom she held a steady affection. Gramps had probed her feelings for him and warned her not to settle down for the sake of security.

But there was no fear of that. It was a platonic friendship, and one she intended keeping that way.

##

The trip home was exhausting–Melissa had to change flights in Brisbane on her way to Armidale. It was dark by the time the taxi dropped her off in front of her semi-detached cottage on the outskirts of town, and she went straight to bed. Rising early the next morning, she shivered as her feet touched the cold floor. Determined to put the events of the last two weeks behind her and get back into her normal routine, she prepared for her morning run. Pulling on a tracksuit and sneakers, she did some stretches before stepping outside. She gasped as her breath misted in the frosty air and pulled a beanie over her head before setting off.

Mrs. McGovern, her neighbour and landlady, was also up early and working in her front garden in the frosty morning.

"Hey, Mrs. Mac, you'll get frostbite on your fingers!" she called out. I'll pick up Luney and Sylvester on the way back."

Mrs. Mac gave her a wave as Melissa broke into a light jog on the footpath. Breathing in the chilly air, her cheeks tingled from the cold. Autumn leaves crunched underfoot as she picked up the pace and did her circuit across town around the back of the university. She was surprised to see two cars and a large black motorcycle parked outside the history building, even though it was the weekend. Two men came out of the building. One of them gave her a quick wave and she waved back, realising it was Professor Andrews.

That must be the new professor with him.

As she jogged around the corner, the motorcycle roared past her and she glanced up, nearly tripping over. The bike rider reminded her of Nick. She tried to push thoughts of him from her mind as she picked up the pace. If every man was going to remind her of him, she had no chance. She had to get over it!

She blocked her holiday from her mind, trying to concentrate on her preparations for her return to work on Monday. By the time she'd completed her circuit, she was warm and had shed her beanie and sweatshirt. Opening the gate to Mrs. Mac's cottage garden, she bent as she caught her breath. The old lady came out of the front door, a birdcage in one hand and a fluffy white cat tucked under her other arm.

"I hope Luney behaved this time. No breakages?" The cat was company for Melissa and kept her entertained with his antics every night as he ran around the apartment. Sylvester, the budgie, chirped as she picked up his cage.

"No worse than usual. Still a mad cat but settling down a bit. She is well named." Mrs. Mac was used to the pets, often minding them for Melissa when she'd travelled down to the coast to visit Gramps.

"By the way, your new neighbour is moving in on the weekend. It's all been organised by the university. I believe he's a new professor."

"Yes," Lissy nodded. "I heard before I went away there is a new professor coming to finish his doctorate and do some lecturing with our faculty. I'm looking forward to meeting him. Let me know if there's anything I can do to help you get the cottage ready. I have the whole weekend free."

Mrs. Mac had split the old bluestone cottage

into two rentals. Lissy loved living in the front half of the old home and helped look after the rambling cottage garden, and often helped out with renovations and odd jobs around both properties.

"I haven't forgotten you want the front fence whitewashed. I've set tomorrow aside for that. Thanks again for minding these two. I'll see you later."

She hurried up the front steps; her phone was ringing. She let herself in the door as she juggled the cat and the birdcage. Putting them down gently in front of the fire, she picked up the phone.

"Melissa McIntyre speaking."

"Hi, darling, just checking you're home safely. How was your trip?" Her mother's voice was bright and happy.

How was the trip? Well, Mum, I learned that foolish behaviour is genetic, and I fell for the first good-looking male who came along. Spent the night with him and moved on. However, I have more sense than you did, and we used protection, so there won't be any lonely children growing up with only one parent.

"Great, thanks, Mum. Got a good tan and I'm relaxed and ready to go back to work."

They chatted for a while and she was surprised to hear her mother and Lars were planning a visit back to Australia in the spring.

"We've timed it with your university session

break, so we can spend some time together at the coast. I have to wrap up some of Gramps' business and get his house sorted."

"It will be great to see you both." She wondered whether Lars would still be on the scene then and if she would even get to meet her latest stepfather. As soon as she ended the call, the phone rang again, and Luney jumped up and started to run around the room.

"Hello." She chuckled as she answered the phone, watching her crazy cat run around the furniture. The budgie chirped in encouragement.

"Hello, Melissa, it's Tom. Welcome home. I'm calling to confirm our date for tonight." Tom Richards was so predictable. He was nice looking, well-mannered, and a stickler for doing the right thing. But his structured life and predictability appealed to her and she always enjoyed their Friday night outing. You couldn't call it a date; they just enjoyed the same movies and food.

"Yes, looking forward to it. It's good to be home and back to normal." There was no way she would share her holiday stories with him this time.

Tom hesitated and cleared his throat.

"Melissa, I was wondering if it would greatly inconvenience you if we changed our routine this week."

They usually dined at Ivy Cottage, a restaurant on the river, and had met there at seven o'clock each Friday night for the past six months, often followed by a movie, apart from the occasions Tom was away on business trips or Melissa was down the coast visiting Gramps.

"There's a family dinner at my parents' home tonight that I must attend, as my brother is coming, and we have all been summoned to the family home." He sounded nervous. "Not that I don't want to go, of course I do, but I was looking forward to our dinner and seeing you. I missed you while you were away."

She was surprised. Tom didn't usually touch on anything personal, and it was most unusual for them to have a conversation like that. She hadn't even known that his family lived in town.

"I would love for you to come with me. It would be a great opportunity to meet my family, while we are all together. It doesn't happen often. I'll pick you up at your place, if that suits you?"

Lissy hesitated. The emotional rollercoaster of the past few weeks had left her feeling fragile, and although it would be nice to meet Tom's family and see him in his comfort zone, she didn't want him to think there was anything more in their relationship. She'd make sure he knew that, so she made a quick decision and spoke before she could change her mind.

"Okay, I'll look forward to it. Is it formal or casual?"

He laughed. "Very casual. I will apologise for my family in advance. Er ... Melissa, there is also something I would like to discuss with you before we get there, so I'll come over about five?"

She felt a rush of affection for Tom. He had shown more emotion in this short conversation than he had in the six months she'd known him. He had been a steady friend as she eased into her new position at the university, and although he was always businesslike and fostered that image with his dress and attention to his personal appearance, she enjoyed his company.

She began to look forward to the evening and sang along with the radio as she went hunting through her wardrobe for something suitably casual to wear. She felt happier than she had since Gramps's death. Sylvester chirped along with her and Luney gave them both a disdainful look as she stretched out on the sunny windowsill washing herself. Lissy laid out a light wool suit in forest green, with her ankle-length boots, before settling down to reading through her notes for work on Monday morning. She wanted to be up-to-date and well prepared for the new professor; he would have some input into her promotion.

She had worked hard at her research to become the youngest lecturer in the history faculty at the small, rural university. Word was out that she was being seriously considered in the current round for a promotion to senior lecturer and it would be an achievement to get that promotion at her age.

A whole new life was about to open up for her.

Chapter Five

Tom arrived at Melissa's front door at precisely five o'clock. Her hair was confined in an elegant French roll and pearl studs in her ears finished off the sedate look. Nice and understated for meeting Tom's family, and casual holidaymaker Lissy's beach clothes were packed away until the next trip to the coast. She ignored the ripple that tingled through her when she thought of the holiday.

No! Back to sedate Melissa, all ready for work.

She ushered Tom in from the cold and was surprised when he pulled a large bunch of roses from behind his back. Reaching over, he kissed her on both cheeks and handed her the flowers. Feeling surprised and a little bit off balance, she hugged the roses to her chest. Tom had never kissed her cheek before, let alone bought her flowers. They even went Dutch at their weekly dinners.

"Thank you, Tom. How thoughtful of you."

"Welcome home. I really missed you." His voice was happy. "You look wonderful. Great tan.

Did you have a good break?"

Lissy hadn't told any of her colleagues about her grandfather's death. As in all aspects of her life she kept herself private and professional at the university. She nodded, smiled and attempted to regain her composure. She wasn't sure about this newly confident and casual Tom. "I'll get a vase from the kitchen. Would you like a drink? I have some white wine in the fridge."

"A small one, please."

Luney jumped down from the chair and wrapped herself around Tom's ankles. Tom picked up the cat and moved across to the fire as Lissy went to the kitchen. Returning with a tray holding a bottle of wine and two glasses, she was pleased to see him sitting on the long settee in front of the fire, stroking Luney. She sat down next to them and placed the tray on the low table between the settee and the fire. Tom poured the wine and held his glass up to hers.

"Cheers," he said. A fleeting image of a tall, tanned sailor flitted through her mind as she looked back at him. Similar eyes, similar cheekbones.

God, she was seeing Nick everywhere in her imagination. Last night, the guy on a toilet paper ad on the television had even looked like him.

Tom fidgeted in his seat and straightened his already perfectly straight tie. Luney jumped across to Lissy's lap when he cleared his throat.

"Is everything all right?" she asked. "Everything's fine at work?"

"Yes." Tom turned and sat up even straighter. "I have something to ask you and I don't know how to go about it."

She tilted her head to the side and smiled at him, he was worked up about something.

"We are really great friends and I know how you feel about love and marriage." He paused and cleared his throat. "I have always had a life plan and I would like to get married and have a family. I intend to do that before I am thirty-five ... get married, that is. What I am trying to find out, Melissa, is if you would be interested in considering my proposition."

"Proposition?" A giggle rose in her throat and she fought it back. She mustn't have heard him right.

"I suppose you could call it a proposal in a way. I don't really mean a proposal, but just suggesting that maybe you give it some thought."

"Give what some thought?" Melissa screwed her nose up as she stared at him.

"Maybe that you get to think of me in the light of a future life partner. Come and meet my family tonight and then we will discuss it again next Friday night."

Melissa was speechless. But poor Tom looked really anxious. Reaching over, she took both of his hands. "Hey, I'm so flattered that you'd consider me as your partner, but this is not us. You know that."

He sighed and eventually agreed. "I know."

"What's happened to bring this on, Tom?"

"Something happened, and I got thinking. Maybe you can learn to love me. And then if and when it comes time for me to turn this proposition into a real proposal, perhaps on bended knee, you will have had time to think about it. I've always thought romantic love was overrated. If you're wise you choose your marriage partner sensibly."

"You know what my grandfather used to say?"

He shook his head.

"Wait for your destiny, and don't settle for less." Gramps had actually made her promise that she would, but there was no need for Tom to know that. "And okay, so you said something happened?"

A glum expression crossed his face as he nodded. "Jill's back."

"Your old girlfriend?"

He nodded again.

"And this has led to this conversation how?"

This time it was an out-of-character shrug. "I guess I got thinking about how she dumped me and how I was going to reach my life plan by thirty-five."

This time Melissa let the laugh bubble out.

"Oh, Tom, you are so precious. But you know we're just friends. Tell me honestly, have you ever had one romantic thought about me?"

His lips tilted in a smile. "No. We're good mates."

"Good, let's leave it there and finish our wine and forget about your 'proposition'." His shoulders relaxed and she realised how nervous he'd been. She reached over and gently kissed his cheek.

"Now let's go so I can meet your family." As she stood up, she had a worrying thought. "You haven't mentioned your proposition to them, have you?"

"No, they know you're my friend from the university."

Tom had a luxury car, an imported British saloon in a silver grey, which suited him, and Lissy loved the feel of the leather upholstery against her legs. They drove a short distance out of town past beautiful old houses, crossed the river; and then he turned through an ornate set of gates, opening to a long drive lined by huge trees. It was a massive double-storey home, and iron lace edged an upstairs veranda that wrapped around the whole house. She counted five chimneys.

"This is absolutely beautiful," she said. "It must be one of the original settler homesteads."

Tom nodded. "It's almost as old as

Saumarez Homestead on the Uralla road. This one was built in 1900 by my father's grandparents and it's been in our family for over a hundred years."

After he parked his car in a carport adjoining the side of the main house, he reached over and took Lissy's hand. "Now, don't be nervous. Dom coming home today has brought the whole family together for the first time for ages."

Melissa patted her hair into place and took a deep breath. She could do a lot worse than Tom, if she was honest, and God knows, after the last week, she was even more convinced of the dangers of physical attraction, and how unwary romantics could be easily ensnared.

A marriage based on common sense and friendship mightn't be such a bad idea.

She shook her head as Gramps's voice circled in her thoughts. She took another deep breath, squared her shoulders, and followed Tom into the fray to meet his family.

He ushered Melissa across a wide veranda at the back of the house that was cluttered with shoes, garden tools, potted plants, and bags of potting mix. He opened a heavy timber door leading into a warm kitchen that was suffused with the golden light of the setting sun. The aroma of baking bread and garlic surrounded them, as did a cacophony of noise. Pausing in the doorway, Melissa watched Tom push past a pair of arguing children, slap the back of a young man talking into a mobile phone, and then plant a noisy kiss on the cheek of the elegant woman standing by the stove.

"Mama, *deliziosa* ... what are we eating tonight?" Tom leaned forward to lift the lid and peer into the bubbling pot on the stove.

Melissa hadn't known that Tom's background was Italian, and she'd never heard him speak the language before. His voice was full of life as he spoke.

"Tomas, where are your manners?" she said, slapping his hand away. "Who is this lovely young woman you bring to my kitchen?" Mrs. Richards was a tall woman, with a tumble of black curls held back loosely with a checked ribbon. She came across to Melissa, wiping her hands on her bright red apron.

"You are Melissa. I am so happy to finally meet you. Please, call me Tessa. Tomas has been very remiss in not bringing you over before; we have heard all about you and your good influence on him."

"Yes, you've gotten him away from his desk and his numbers," interjected the young man as he put his mobile in his pocket.

"Alex, don't be rude!"

"Yes, Mama." He grinned widely at Tom and Melissa. "Welcome. You do you know you're too beautiful for my ugly old brother? Why don't you run away with me instead?"

"I'm not running away with anyone." Melissa smiled and took Tessa's outstretched hands. "It was very kind of you to invite me tonight, since I know it's a special family dinner. I feel welcome already."

Tessa broke into a wide smile. "Tonight, our second son, Dominic will be home from his work in the Cook Islands, and we are all together for the first time in three years. It is a very special night. Now, Tomas, take Melissa into the living room. Your sisters are in there."

Tom ushered her into a beautiful room that seemed to be full of children and was as noisy as the kitchen. Lissy felt overwhelmed by the noise and the number of adults and children sprawled on lounges and on the floor in front of the crackling open fire. Tom spread his arms in a wide gesture and said proudly, "*la mia famiglia* – my family."

She experienced a surge of true affection for Tom. He was so obviously a part of this boisterous and loving family. Tom, in his family setting, was very different from the polite and shy accountant she dined with on Friday nights. She smothered a smile as Alex followed them into the room.

"Come on you old stuffed shirt, you don't have to impress anyone here," he said as he undid Tom's tie and flung it on the table.

"Enough, enough! Your manners,

Alessandro." Tessa picked up the tie and handed it back to Tom. "Take the children outside and run off some of your energy, so we can introduce Melissa in peace."

"Yes, Mama," said Alex, with a twinkle in his eye. "Come on kids, a quick game of cricket before Uncle Dom arrives. First one outside gets to bat." He winked at Lissy as he ran out to the veranda followed by half a dozen children of various ages and sizes.

Even after Alex led the children outside through the French doors, the room stayed noisy. Lissy was fascinated and looked around the elegant but welcoming room. A cricket game was blaring from the huge television on the far wall as three men loudly criticised the failure of a fieldsman to take a catch. Two beautiful babies with big blue eyes were yelling as they climbed over their respective mothers' legs.

"Quiet, please. Girls, this is Melissa." Tom had to raise his voice over the din in the room. "My three little sisters, Sophie, Allie, and Lucy."

Lissy greeted them as Tom moved on to introduce their assorted husbands and the two babies still in the room, and Alex's fiancée, Emily. In the middle of the introductions, a huge golden retriever came bounding through the room chased by two small boys, almost knocking Lissy from her feet. She fell into the chair behind her as Sophie,

Tom's oldest sister, chastised the boys.

"Be careful!" She turned to Lissy and laughed. "Welcome to our madhouse!"

"Thanks," said Lissy, settling into the chair and following the different conversations with interest. She was immediately included as though she was a part of the family and felt welcome and comfortable even though she was in a room full of strangers. She recalled Gramps's comments. *Maybe I have found my destiny. Maybe Tom was under my nose the whole time and I didn't appreciate him.* She looked across at Tom watching the cricket game with his brother-in-law, trying to imagine herself in an embrace with him. As hard as she tried, Nick kept pushing into her thoughts and she shook herself in annoyance.

"Is everything all right?" Tom leaned towards her, a look of concern on his face.

"I'm sorry?" She realised she had spoken her thoughts aloud and Tom was sitting next to her on the lounge. She felt her cheeks grow rosy and reached for her glass of water on the table, as excited cries drifted in from the back garden.

"Yes, I'm fine," she said.

"Uncle Dom's here!" The throaty roar of a motorcycle coming up the driveway drowned out the excited squeals of the children.

"Thanks!" Lissy found herself with two babies unceremoniously dropped on her knees as the three sisters jumped up and ran out through the French doors to the driveway.

Tessa ran through the living room like a young girl, her black curls tumbling from the ribbon. Tom reached over and took one of the babies from her lap.

"Sorry, I did try to warn you about this mad lot, but they are in even finer form tonight with Dom coming home. Once Mama assures herself that he is really home and in one piece, things will settle down and we'll probably have a relatively civilised meal." There was a flurry of noise and movement as the children ran back inside, chattering with excitement, followed closely by the adults.

"Uncle Dom, did you bring us any presents? Any shrunken heads?"

Lissy looked at Tom and laughed. "Shrunken heads?"

"It's a common occurrence. I don't know if I mentioned to you that Dom is the new professor in the history faculty. He's been doing research in the South Pacific for the last two years and has come home to write up his thesis and do some lecturing in the undergraduate Pacific history course. He's always sending gruesome bits and pieces to our nephews and they love it."

"He's going to be in our faculty." Lissy looked up at him, surprised. "Mrs. Mac, my landlady, was talking about him this morning. He's moving into the other flat in the cottage. I didn't realise he was your brother."

"Mama won't be happy about that. I think she hoped he would stay at home for a while, although I can understand why he wants his own place. The noise level here tonight is normal and there wouldn't be much chance of getting his thesis written."

Lissy stood up and shifted the baby to her hip, and small chubby hands reached out and grabbed a handful of her hair. Tom placed one hand gently on her neck as he untangled the baby's hand from the bunch of curls he had pulled from her clip. His body blocked her view of the newcomer and her heart almost stopped as she heard a familiar deep voice.

"Tomas, a girlfriend and a baby? About time!" Tom turned around laughing as he grabbed his brother in a huge hug with lots of affectionate backslapping. "Girlfriend maybe, but this is Sophie's third-born, you idiot."

Lissy turned in shock and her head spun as she looked up into familiar blue eyes. Dom's attention shifted to her, and the tight smile on his face sent a chill shivering down her spine as she struggled to keep a firm hold on the baby and fight the dizziness blurring her vision.

She felt her heart thump and then race.

My God! How wonderful, and bizarre, to see

Nick again, even though he looked surprised, even angry. She opened her mouth to say hello but was interrupted by Tom.

"Dom, this is Melissa McIntyre, a friend of mine from the university. Melissa just told me that you'll be working in her faculty."

Nick reached over and took Lissy's free hand in his as she carefully juggled the baby on her hip. "What a coincidence," he drawled. "Delighted to meet you, *Melissa*."

She turned and handed the baby back to Sophie as Tessa came over and clapped her hands, inviting everyone to make their way out to dinner. The room began to clear as the family followed Nick outside and she took the opportunity to dash to the bathroom.

Wide-eyed, she raised trembling fingers to her cheeks as she looked into the mirror and saw the pallor beneath her tan. She pinched her cheeks before running cold water over her wrists.

What was the probability of Nick—*Nick* from her holiday fling—being the new professor in her history faculty at the university? And the brother of her friend who had come up with a stupid proposition tonight? And her new neighbour? The coincidences were staggering at best.

She groaned and fought to pull herself together. How typical. It proved to her once again that you didn't trust physical attraction under the moonlight. Not only was Nic a liar—his name was Dom, he'd even lied about his name—he was going to be her new boss! And on top of that, he would be the one with the final say in her promotion.

You can kiss that good-bye, Dr. McIntyre.

##

Gas heaters lined the wall to ward off the New England chill and Melissa moved to the dark end of the table, away from the heat. Sitting down, she watched Nick hugging his mother at the other end of the table.

I know how good those arms feel. Closing her eyes, she remembered him holding her close. Had that really happened only two nights ago?

She was hot, despite the chill in the air, and her heart was still pumping hard and fast. Reaching for the carafe of water, she poured herself a glass, the ice cubes tinkling as her hands shook. She was so angry at his lack of acknowledgement that they'd already met in the islands, she felt as though sparks should be jumping from her. He had made her a liar too, with his omission, and she hadn't had time to query it.

"Are you okay? I hope my family hasn't overwhelmed you?" Tom frowned and leaned close as he sat next to her. Nick was watching from the other end of the table and she deliberately put her hand up to touch Tom's face.

Stuff Nick. Let him think what he wants.

"It's absolutely wonderful. Being an only child, I've never been part of such a big family celebration before."

Tom seemed surprised at her touching his face but he put his hand over hers. "You're welcome to visit whenever you want. I didn't realise you have no family around."

Melissa looked down the table. Nick's expression was cold and aloof as he met her gaze. She was going to have to cut ties with this family to save her sanity. Her feelings in chaos, she longed for the evening to be over, so she could escape.

"What do you specialise in at the university, Melissa?" Nick had moved down the table and had taken a chair in between two of his sisters, across from her and Tom.

"Pacific history," she said. She put her head down and fiddled with her hair clip.

"Interesting. You don't look like a girl who would know anything about history. Glorious hair, by the way. I hope my brother has told you how ravishing you look this evening. What a fabulous suntan." His eyes blatantly ran over her, completely different to the gentle way he had looked at her only a couple of nights before. She froze, frightened she would lose her temper and make a rude comment, but Tessa rescued her.

"Stop teasing. You and Alex are incorrigible. No wonder poor Tom rarely brings anyone home. Behave while I retrieve your father from the study. He's so immersed in his new book, that he hasn't even heard you arrive."

Nick leaned back and gave his mother another kiss on the cheek as she walked past.

"It's okay, Mama. Melissa and I will get to know each other at the university. I'm sure she'll get used to me." Lissy looked across at him and saw his eyes glittering with a promise of things to come.

##

It seemed the night went on forever. She met Professor Richards senior, who had been firmly ensconced in his study through all the excitement of Nick arriving, and had sat bemused as a procession of aunts, uncles, cousins and neighbours dropped in to greet Nick. Word had spread that the Pacific adventurer was home. She met so many people, her head spun and the effort of keeping calm and friendly was making her feel ill. All night she was conscious of Nick's simmering mood. She had learned to read him so well in such a short time. She sat quietly, and only spoke when someone included her in a conversation. Not only had he left her that final morning on Hamilton Island without so much as a good-bye or see you later, the coward had slipped out in the darkness.

And lied about his name, so she couldn't find him.

Talk about wham, bam, thank you ma'am.

And the lying sailor was actually a university professor. And one she was going to have to work with.

Lissy sat there alternating between feeling hot and cold and considered Nick's deception. Her jaw ached from clenching her teeth. Her mood must have been obvious because Tom offered to drive her home.

"No, call me a taxi. Enjoy the rest of the night and catch up with your brother." She said her good-byes to the family after he reluctantly agreed and called the local taxi company.

"It was wonderful to finally meet you. I do hope Tomas brings you again soon," said Tessa, enfolding Lissy in a warm embrace. Tom's sisters all gave her hugs as she made her way through the living room, where children of various ages were asleep on cushions on the floor. Nick followed Tom and Lissy out to the front veranda, as Alex yelled out to Tom.

"When's the wedding, big brother? You're almost thirty-five."

Tessa glared at Alex and turned to Lissy. "Once again, I apologise for my sons, they have no manners. They take after their father."

Professor Richards gravely shook her hand and Lissy was sure he didn't even know who she was in the procession of visitors who had been through the house that evening. With a great sense of relief, she saw the lights of the taxi as it pulled up in the driveway. She gave Tom a brief hug and a light kiss on the cheek.

"I'll give you a call next week about Friday night," he said.

Nick appeared behind them.

"Goodnight, Melissa," he said, emphasizing the second half of her name. "I'll see you on Monday at work. I'm really looking forward to getting to know you better."

"Me too, I can't wait to hear about your adventures in the Pacific, *Dominic*," she said, emphasizing the Nic in his name. Tom opened the door of the taxi and she slid across the seat, her hands over her eyes.

Why the hell didn't we just laugh and say we had already met? What a fine mess I'm in, so much for destiny. Not only do I have to put up with him at work, he's going to be living on the other side of my cottage. Wait until he finds out about that coincidence!

That was about the only thing that made her smile. She knew he wasn't going to like that.

***

Nick stood silently on the stairs watching the taillights of the taxi disappear down the driveway. Tom walked up the stairs towards his brother, his movements precise and considered, like everything else he did.

"Well?"

"Well, what?" replied Nick, knowing his brother wanted him to say how great Melissa was.

"What did you think of Melissa?"

Nick tried to think of a suitable reply as they went back to the veranda.

"Great. Very pretty." He turned and thumped Tom on the back. "Come on, mate, enough of women tonight. You know me...love 'em and leave 'em." He reached into the refrigerator and threw his older brother a can of beer. "You and I have a lot of catching up to do."

He was cranky with himself because he'd been so attracted to Lissy on the island, and then he'd slept with her. He felt bad because he'd scarpered out of her room before she woke up the next morning because the response he'd had to her was something way out of his experience.

It had scared him, and like a fool he'd thought it was easier to make himself scarce. Serious relationships weren't for him, and he didn't know what he was going to say to her.

Maybe he was being old fashioned. Maybe it had been just casual sex to her.

And what the hell was she doing up there, sleeping with him if she was Tom's girlfriend? He'd had a lucky escape, and somehow, he was going to have to warn Tom.

Women. They were all the same.

Not to be trusted. Ever. With the exception of his mother and sisters, of course.

Tom caught the beer and leaned against the railing.

"Tell me about your latest trip. Did you get your research finished ... are you happy to be back at the university? You don't look very impressed."

"You know me," replied Nick. "I prefer to be on the Islands, but I have to spend some time at the university or the funding for my projects would dry up." He turned and looked out into the darkness and shivered as the late night breeze picked up. "I don't know how you cope, going to the same boring office, day in, day out."

Tom sighed and made an admission that startled Nick. "You know, if I'm honest? I was starting to get a bit bored with it but having Melissa as a friend has livened up my life."

Nick grunted.

"I asked her to consider a future with me when I picked her up tonight. But—"

"She's not your type." Nick knew his voice was short. Tom had always needed his approval, even though Nick was younger than him. Well, this time, for his own good, he'd have to do without it. He pushed himself away from the railing and tried to ignore the lump that seemed to have settled in his throat. "I've had enough to drink. I'm going to bed."

"Night, bro." Tom reached over and enveloped him in a bear hug. "It's great to have you home, even if it will only be for a short while."

Nick kept the smile on his face even though he wanted to drag his hands down his face in frustration.

Sleep eluded him for a long time. What were the odds of Lissy being on his staff, two thousand miles from the playground of the Whitsunday Islands, and with her eyes firmly set on Tom? She had thought Nick was a drifter, and to top it all off, he'd slept with her. He had to forget that night. There was nowhere for it to go. He would work with her and get the project finished and return to the Islands as quickly as he could.

Chapter Six

Lissy hoped to fall into oblivion the moment her head touched the pillow, but the events of the night kept her tossing and turning into the early hours. Waking late, she got up in a very sour mood. Her eyes were scratchy from lack of sleep. Sipping her coffee in the kitchen, she watched Luney run around and knock over the pile of kindling next to the old combustion stove. The mad cat's antics added to her bad mood and she banished the cat to the laundry room.

She decided to work off her mood by getting an early start on whitewashing the cottage fence. Changing into her oldest shorts and sweatshirt, she tied her curls back with a bandana and then collected the painting gear from the laundry cupboard.

"Sorry, Luney, it's not your fault I'm so grumpy this morning." Melissa stepped out into the old cottage garden, which was bursting with the bronze and gold of late autumn, the leaves crunching underfoot as she walked across to the fence. Kneeling down on the footpath outside the garden fence, she opened the bucket of whitewash and began to paint the old timber. The rhythmic motion of the brush going up and down the palings did nothing to soothe her mood as she simmered over the events of the previous evening.

Thoughts of revenge flitted through her mind as she pictured a variety of punishments suitable for Nick. By the time she was halfway along the front panel of the fence, he had walked the gangplank, been clapped in irons, tied to the mast, and marooned on one of his tropical islands. Yes, marooning sounded good, preferably on an isolated island a long way from her.

The roar of a motorcycle thundering up the quiet street interrupted her fantasy. Putting the brush in the paint tin, she turned around and stood, hands on her hips, as Nick turned into the driveway and cut the engine. He swaggered over to her, his eyes snapping with anger.

"Good morning, *Melissa*." Throwing the helmet aside, he bent down so that his eyes were level with hers. "Or is Lissy back this morning in the sexy shorts? Who will I be living with? Lissy or Melissa?"

"You won't be living with either!" She stepped away from him. There was a loud clatter as she backed into the paint, knocking the bucket over and white paint splattered up the backs of her legs.

"Now look what you've done!" Bending down, she set the bucket upright, looking around for something to wipe the paint from her legs. Swearing to herself, she pulled the bandana from her hair and her curls cascaded around her face as she scrubbed furiously at her legs.

Nic stood back, looking her up and down, a tight smile on his face.

"Well, we definitely have Lissy back. Fascinating how you move so easily from one to the other."

"You are full of it, Dominic." She threw the paint-soaked bandana to the ground and picked up the paintbrush. "What happened to Nic, the sailor?"

He ignored her question. "Demure Melissa, what a lovely wife she would have made for Tom. I bet he hasn't met the free and easy Lissy," he said.

"How dare you pass judgment on me. What about you, *Dominic*? Just thrill seeking around the Pacific for a few years, professor? Having a few bets and picking up any gullible female for a bit of fun and sneaking out before they could find out the truth? Or is that just a line you use to make you more attractive to anyone who doesn't fall for the 'angel face' line straight up?" She stepped towards him, emphasizing each word with the paintbrush. Dollops of white paint flicked on to his face and black T-shirt. He grabbed her wrist and held the brush above her head.

"I don't want my brother hurt by a cheating girlfriend again." Nick's voice was getting louder. "The elegant suit and fancy hairdo may suck him in, but I know a hypocrite from a hundred yards away. Trust me, I've had lots of experience."

"Oh, I'm sure," she said between gritted teeth, as she tried to ignore the crazy little flutters that were travelling up her arm from where he held her.

Hurried footsteps and a concerned voice stopped them both in their tracks.

"Is everything okay?" Mrs. Mac stood on her front porch. She looked taken aback as if she sensed the tension in the air. "I was just going out when I heard your voices."

Lissy carefully removed the paintbrush from Nick's hands and turned to Mrs. Mac. "Oh, it's okay, Professor Richards came to collect his key and I accidentally flicked him with paint. He was helping me with the brush. It was so nice of him."

Mrs. Mac didn't look convinced that the man clad in black leathers and a T-shirt towering over Lissy could be a professor. Nick stepped forward with his hand outstretched, giving the older woman the benefit of his devastating smile.

"Mrs. Mac, I'm delighted to meet you." He held her little wrinkled hands between his, and Melissa rolled her eyes. "Please call me Nick. I signed all the paperwork at the university yesterday and I believe I'm supposed to collect the key here."

Lissy watched Nick put on the charm and saw its immediate impact on their elderly landlady as she fell under his spell. He saw her expression and responded with a brilliant grin, and, despite her anger, she felt the inevitable tug to her heartstrings.

"It's okay, I've still got the spare keys inside. I'll show the professor through his side of the cottage," Melissa said. Looking a lot happier, Mrs. Mac bid them farewell and headed towards her little car. Melissa's shoulders slumped in defeat. "You had better come inside and get cleaned up, and then I'll show you your half of the cottage."

Nick looked at her closely and she knew that the tension of the past few days was visible in the dark shadows under her eyes. Sighing, she turned, and he followed her up the steps into the laundry. Handing him a washcloth to clean the paint from his face, she went into the kitchen to collect his keys.

She reached over for the keys on the hook and turned, bumping into a rock-hard chest. She stepped back, but he took a step closer and warm hands gripped her shoulders.

"We have a problem here, Lissy. Simple fact ... I want you out of the picture with my brother." He paused, and she could hear the frustration in his voice.

"So how is that a problem?" His eyes were holding hers intently and she found it hard to look away."

"Because if I'm honest, I don't want you out of the picture … my picture. Despite common sense and logic, you fascinate me. Can you explain that to me?"

Her heart began to pound. "No, I can't," she said with a sad weariness.

He pulled her closer. "Let me show you." His head tilted down towards her and she watched as his lips parted, and quite suddenly, Lissy felt anger take over her whole body. The range of emotions she had experienced since she had first seen Nick swinging down from the mast of the yacht coalesced into pure black rage. She pulled away and shoved him.

"You know nothing, *nothing* about me! How dare you stand there and tell me I'm not good enough for your brother. And then tell me you want me! You've got a nerve."

Turning away from him, she lowered her voice. "Go away and leave me alone. Go look at your cottage. Move in, bring in a harem for all I care. I don't care what you do, just leave me alone."

"You confuse me," he replied softly.

"I want you to leave, now." Her voice was firm. "I have work to do."
She walked across and opened the door.

"Lissy, Melissa, I mean. Come with me and show me the cottage." He ran his fingers through his shaggy hair in frustration. "You live here. I've signed the lease. We have to sort this out. Come on, let's pretend this is the first time we've met and you're showing me my new rental. I won't touch you again."

But how much did she want him to?

She stood, without answering for a short time, then squared her shoulders and answered him. "I'll show you around only if you promise not to have any contact with me once you move in, apart from work."

"Fine," he said carefully, moving around her to go out to the veranda. As he walked past the laundry window, a lazy paw swiped out at him, lightly scratching his forearm.

Melissa reached over and gave the white cat a quick rub on the head. "Nick, meet Luney, she'll keep you on the straight and narrow."

***

The entrance to the other side of the cottage was at the far end of the front veranda. Nick followed Lissy as she unlocked the door; they entered an airy room bathed in sunshine. An open fireplace bore testimony to the cold New England evenings.

"You'll have to set up a firewood delivery. I can give you the phone number," she said. Even her damn voice was attractive.

"Thank you," he said, moving into the next room.

"It's a mirror image of my side." Lissy moved quickly through the rooms. "Two bedrooms. I use one for a study, a separate dining room and the small bathroom and laundry."

She went through the cottage showing him the basics. As she turned to go back toward the living room Lissy stumbled over a loose piece of carpet. Nick put out his hand and caught her before she could fall. His elbow brushed the softness of her breast and his arm automatically went around her waist. He groaned and pulled her into a close embrace. His face was almost level with hers and he could see the deep green flecks in her eyes. He ran his hands through her wild curls and remembered the pleasure of her hair on his body that one night they'd spent together.

Nick's heart was thumping hard. Despite knowing that he should not touch her, his heart was telling him a different story. Looking down into her eyes, he saw a small smile playing around her lips as she touched the flecks of white paint on his chin. He lowered his mouth to hers and closed his eyes revelling in the sensation of her soft lips opening under his.

He pulled her closer, oblivious to anything as she whimpered with pleasure and then realisation kicked in for him. He had never lost control like this before. Lissy stiffened in his arms and it was like a trigger back to reality for him. He pulled away from her. He had never felt like this before and it unsettled him.

Years ago, Olivia had thrown his love back at him as though he had not meant anything to her. Even then, he'd never lost control like this.

Damn her! He had not fallen for a woman since then, and he was not about to start now.

"You are really clever, aren't you?" he said. "You know what you want, and you go for it, don't you?"

Her open palm hit his cheek with a crack that moved his head sideways and left his cheek stinging.

"You sanctimonious bastard!" She threw the house keys at him and stalked from the room, slamming the door behind her. He watched her go, his blood still pounding from kissing her.

Chapter Seven

Melissa spent a lonely weekend ignoring the flurry of activity, the removalist truck and assorted vehicles that pulled into the driveway. A couple of times someone knocked on her door, but she turned up her music and ignored the knocking. An occasional glance from her window confirmed that most of the Richards family had arrived to help Nick at some point over the two days. Late on Sunday afternoon, Luney meowed incessantly at the door until Lissy let her out.

"Traitor," she murmured when Luney ran to Nick as he carried boxes across the back garden.

She worked hard at regaining her equilibrium on Sunday, keeping herself busy cleaning out cupboards and avoiding her new neighbour. Each time his face appeared in her mind—as it did most of the day—she deliberately blocked him from her thoughts. By the time darkness fell, she had calmed down and as the night chill slipped in, she split some kindling on the veranda. As soon as she had a fire going, she indulged in a hot bubble bath and put on her flannel Mickey Mouse pyjamas.

"Okay, time for work," she muttered as she opened her briefcase and read over the research notes she had left unfinished before going to Gramps's funeral. Even though she was aware of an occasional noise through the wall, she managed to concentrate on her research for a couple of hours and kept thoughts of Nick and his close proximity at bay. When her eyelids began to droop, and she couldn't hold back the yawn any longer, she packed her notes up ready for her return to work in the morning. Looking around for Luney, she realised the cat was still outside. She went to the door to let her inside but there was no sign of the cat.

Don't tell me another female has fallen for the irresistible professor, she thought with disgust. Pulling on her boots and grabbing a thick coat off the laundry hook, she went out to the veranda, softly calling to the missing feline.

Damn cat, she thought as she moved across the lawn, the frost crunching under her boots. Standing by the fence, she stood still and continued to call Luney. A sliver of light appeared on the back veranda; Nick's back door opened and the light shining from inside the cottage silhouetted his tall figure.

She eased back into the shadows near the fence. The old swing seat on the veranda creaked as

Nick settled into it. The chill wind blowing from the west sent a flurry of dry leaves skittering across the path near the gate. If she stayed outside much longer, she would freeze. A white streak of movement near the fence alerted her to Luney's whereabouts and the mad cat sat down at her feet, meowing loudly. Knowing that Nick would see her as she crossed the lawn to go back in, she gathered the folds of her coat with as much dignity as she could muster and strode out across the grass, calling the cat to follow her up the back steps.

Nick was sitting legs outstretched, arms akimbo, looking relaxed. He reached out and grabbed her hand as she attempted to slip past him.

"Lissy, we need to talk."

"What about?" Her words were clipped, and she pulled away from him, trying to escape the warmth of the fingers grasping hers.

"Living here together, working together, setting some ground rules."

"I don't need any rules. Living here was fine until you rode into town on your noisy motorbike." She glared at him.

"You can't stay bunkered down in your half of the cottage forever. This is the first time you've been outside all weekend."

"Been spying on me, have you? You keep to your side, I'll keep to mine. I'm sure we'll pass occasionally in the corridors at the university, but that's it. You think I'm smart? Well, I am. Smart enough to keep out of your way."

She knew her voice was angry, but she was. Angry, that was. Angry that he thought so poorly of her.

It took two to tango.

Nick stood and let her hand go, burying his own hands in his coat pockets. She backed away from him and turned towards her door.

"Lissy—"

"No, don't you dare call me that. You want rules. Well, the first rule is you call me Melissa or Dr. McIntyre. Second one, you keep your distance from me. Third, you keep your hands off me."

She bent down and picked up Luney, who was winding around her legs. Pushing past Nick on the narrow veranda, she walked to her back door. He made no move to stop her and she didn't look at him as she closed the door firmly behind her.

***

Melissa had slept like the dead for the first time in a week and woke in a panic when she realised she was going to be late on her first day back at work. Getting dressed as quickly as she could and skipping her morning coffee, she ran to her car and drove across town to the university.

Grabbing a coffee from the cafe, she was greeted by two colleagues from her faculty.

After a chat about her holiday, she said to

her friend, Jenny. "I'm thinking of taking some leave."

"More leave? You just got back, Melissa." Jenny knew her well enough to know when something was bothering her. "Is everything okay? Why do you need more leave?"

"Anyway," chimed in Clare. "The head of faculty has cancelled all leave applications until the current budget period is over. That's three months away. Besides, who wants to leave now? You should see the new professor. Everyone's been running around this morning trying to get a glimpse of him. Talk about a hunk. Roared up the drive on a big black motorcycle. Drop dead gorgeous ... looks like he just stepped out of a *Pirates of the Caribbean* movie."

Melissa pulled a face as Jenny hurried them along. "Come on, gals, we have to be in the conference room in five minutes for a faculty meeting."

She hurried to her office, juggling her handbag, briefcase, laptop and coffee before she placed them on the floor next to the door. Her hands shook as she pinned up a couple of curls that had come loose. Using the mirror behind the door of her office, she reapplied her lipstick before picking up her laptop and coffee and heading for the conference room.

Most of the faculty were already seated at

the round conference table and several of her colleagues greeted her as she hurried past. She found a vacant seat at the far end of the table just as Professor Andrews, the head of the history faculty, entered the room, accompanied by the new associate professor.

She took a deep breath, determined to remain calm and professional as Clare kicked her under the table.

"See what I mean," she whispered. "Johnny Depp look-alike." Lissy scowled at her.

"You're incorrigible. Besides, Johnny Depp has dark hair and a moustache in the pirate movies!"

As Professor Andrews called for quiet, Lissy sat back and caught Nick looking down the table directly at her. His hair *was* darker, as the sun-bleached thatch had been trimmed to a neat short back and sides since she had last seen him. The relaxed and easy-going buccaneer had disappeared and in his place was the clean-shaven academic clad in a three-piece suit and tie. She glared at him down the length of the table, and he raised a sardonic brow.

"I would like to welcome you all to this morning's meeting and thank you for interrupting your busy schedules," intoned the deep voice of Professor Andrews. "This morning, Professor Dominic Richards joins our history faculty and we'd like to extend a warm welcome to him. I will introduce him to you individually at the morning tea after the meeting. I'm sure you'll all make him very welcome." He continued with the faculty arrangements for the rest of semester and his monotonous voice fell into the background as Lissy mulled over the situation she found herself in at home, and at work.

I should be able to avoid him for most of the time. I'll do my research in the library, and hopefully, he'll take the vacant office on the next level. I won't go near the Richards' farm, and if there are any faculty social activities, I'll go down to the coast for the weekend and I'll—

"Dr. McIntyre?" she felt another kick to her leg under the table from Clare.

"Dr. McIntyre!" repeated the head of faculty.

"Yes, Professor Andrews?"

"As I was saying, I would like you to meet with myself and Professor Richards after morning tea, to organise the project."

"The project?"

"Yes, Dr. McIntyre, the project." Professor Andrews looked annoyed. "I just finished explaining that the major thrust of our research for the next semester will be related to Professor Richard's Pacific study, and you will be his primary research assistant. We will meet in my office after tea to finalise the arrangements."

"Yes, Professor Andrews." Lissy groaned inwardly and looked down at the table. Clare and Jenny were looking at her with envy. The meeting ended and as the staff moved to the table at the back of the room to the morning tea table, she made for the door.

"Not so fast, Dr. McIntyre." Nick appeared in front of her.

Conscious of the curious looks coming her way, she paused before greeting him politely for the benefit of the staff within earshot. Her words of welcome were aided by the self-control she was exerting. "Welcome to the university, Professor Richards." He took her arm and drew her into the corner. A frisson of warmth lingered where his fingers lightly held her elbow and her heart started to race as she fought the urge to shake his hand off her arm.

"Thank you, Dr. McIntyre. Now, how do you want to play this?" he asked quietly when they were out of earshot. "Will we say we have already met? I don't want you to be embarrassed."

"I am not embarrassed, Professor. I believe we met at your parents' house on Friday evening and then you moved into the cottage next door to me on the weekend if my memory serves me correctly."

"Look, Lissy, even though we had a rocky

start, we still have to work together and socialise—not to mention—live in the same house."

"A rocky start, that's an interesting way to put it." She folded her arms and glared at him, despite the curious looks of her colleagues. "Hmm, let me see. Lying to me, a sexist bet, taking advantage of an innocent tourist. Yep, you could call that a rocky start."

Frustrated, he ran his hand through what was left of his hair. Looking up at him, she was amused to see that there were a couple of stray flecks of white paint remaining in the stubble.

"Look, I'm trying to be the adult here," he said. "We need to sort this out and quickly."

She couldn't help herself as she pointed to his hair. "Been painting, Professor?"

"A run in with a little harridan's paint brush over the weekend." She stared at him and the amusement on his face surprised her. A warm feeling tugged at her tummy.

"Okay, let's call a truce," she said. "I need another coffee. We can talk over that."

They moved across the room to the morning tea table, acting like two colleagues getting to know each other. Nick poured her a cup of coffee in one of the elegant cups provided by the caterers, and Lissy's hand trembled as she held the cup and saucer. Jenny and Clare wandered over and introduced themselves to Nick. Lissy ignored the jealous feeling that ran through her.

Professor Andrews' voice boomed out. "Okay folks, back to work. Lots of planning to be done, and there are students waiting for the ten o'clock lecturers." A couple of academic staff scurried out to their lecture halls as the professor glanced pointedly at his watch.

"Dr. McIntyre, Professor Richards, give me five minutes and come up to my office please," he said.

Lissy made a quick escape as Clare and Jenny kept Nick talking. She entered her office, closed the door, and leaned against it, her eyes closed and heart thudding.

What on earth am I going to do?

Chapter Eight

Taking a deep breath, Lissy turned and looked into the mirror on the back of her door. Even her hair had come loose from its tight French roll, with a couple of curly wisps falling over her flushed cheeks. Her green eyes glittered with emotion. Her legs were shaking and felt as though they wouldn't hold her up.

One look at him and my body goes into meltdown. I will not let him make me feel like this.

With trembling hands, she pinned her hair back and applied fresh lipstick as the memory of their night together filled her thoughts. She swallowed back the tears as she rummaged in her handbag for a rarely-used compact, and then patted a little bit of natural beige powder onto her flushed cheeks. She drank a big glass of water from the cooler in the corner of her office and a semblance of control returned. Picking up her laptop, she headed upstairs to the faculty administration offices.

Nancy, Professor Andrews' secretary, ushered her in, with a huge smile.

"Lovely tan, Melissa. Did you have a nice break?"

After a brief conversation, she entered the large office and joined Professor Andrews and Nick at a low coffee table in the corner.

"Professor Richards has carried out extensive research in the Pacific over the past two years, and we're proud to be associated with his final research paper. Dr. McIntyre, I want you to put your work aside for the rest of the semester and assist the professor with the final research and writing of the report. Your previous research will lead into his perfectly. I anticipate that the paper will acknowledge you as a co-author and that will look magnificent on your curriculum vitae. As you know, there is another associate professorship coming up later this year and you would be well-placed to apply, as co-author of a report of this importance."

Nick sat quietly as Professor Andrews outlined the project to Lissy. He was polite and considerate and showed a keen interest in her previous research, asking several pertinent questions. After they had covered all of the items that the professor raised, she stood to leave.

"Thank you, Professor Andrews, that is a wonderful offer and I will give it serious thought," she said. It was a golden opportunity to advance her academic career. To be an associate professor by thirty would be amazing.

"Dr. McIntyre, you have misunderstood. It is a *fait accompli*," replied Professor Andrews. "One of our new research assistants took over your project while you were on holiday. I have placed Professor Richards in the office next to yours and I expect you to start work together immediately. I am sorry if that inconveniences you." He looked over his glasses at her, not looking the least bit sorry, more confused at her reluctance to take this opportunity.

"I have also cancelled all leave for the rest of the semester as we are under funding pressure to get all of our research papers finalised by then."

Lissy looked at Nick, who was sitting there quietly and turned to Professor Andrews.

"I would be delighted to work with Professor Richards, sir. I am sure we will forge a productive partnership."

Professor Andrews indicated he had another meeting to attend and as they left his office, Nick turned to her.

"Can I see you in your office, Dr. McIntyre?"

"Certainly, give me ten minutes," she said, her face expressionless, as they entered the corridor together.

***

A short time later, Nick tapped lightly on

Lissy's office door, unsure of the welcome he would receive. The damn woman confused him no end. Seeing her at his family home, cosy with Tom, had given him a tight knot in his stomach.

He'd felt her sadness so strongly when they had dinner on Hamilton Island, and even though she seemed to regret their night together, he had no regrets. He'd felt like an utter louse leaving her all rosy and sweetly asleep, but the strong attraction he felt to her had frightened him and he decided he wasn't going to risk his heart again. If he'd known he was going to see her again maybe he would have stayed.

Maybe he would have run a mile.

He ran his hand through his hair, still not used to the short haircut his mother had given him last night. He had gone to the farm on his motorcycle after Lissy had closed the door on him, hoping the ride would clear his head.

"Dominic, you look like a pirate." Tessa tapped his head with the clippers. "You need to look like a professor." He'd enjoyed sitting in front of the fire as his mother cut his hair and caught him up on all the family news.

"What about Tomas, Mama? Is this a serious romance?" he asked casually. Tessa laughed.

"No, I don't think so. Remember Tomas's life plan says marriage at thirty-five and we have a couple of years to go before that. Although, I wouldn't mind. Melissa seems like a very lovely girl."

"Yeah, his list making." Nick chuckled.

"Remember the list on his bedroom wall when he was ten," said Tessa laughing.

"Seven o'clock, wake up, seven fifteen eat breakfast, seven thirty, brush my teeth," they chanted together. Tessa paused, holding the clippers aloft, looking thoughtful.

"I watched Melissa the other night and she looked sad. She was far away in her thoughts a lot of the time during dinner."

Nick bit his tongue; he didn't want any inkling of his relationship with Lissy to get to his brother. Tom had gone out with Olivia before she moved on to Nick, eventually dumping him after all and marrying a rich grazier. Obviously neither of the Richards brothers had measured up financially in those days.

He came back to the present as Lissy called him to come in. He opened the door to the office and walked inside. She sat straight-backed behind her desk and he took a moment to look around her office, noticing a couple of photos on the wall. Beach scenes with two elderly men in the foreground, in front of old fishing boats.

"Take a seat," she said primly. Before he sat, he wandered over and looked closely at the photos.

"Your grandfather and his boat?" he asked gently. He looked at her and was surprised to see the traces of tears on her cheeks. Her lipstick was gone, and she had a tight expression on her face. She nodded and pointed to the chair.

"Where shall we start, Professor? I am not at all familiar with your research."

So that's the way it was going to be. Straight to business.

Her hands were clasped tightly on the desk and he saw the effort she was making to keep her emotions hidden. He sat in the chair opposite her and leaned forward, resting his elbows on his knees as he dropped his head in his hands. Shaking his head, he asked, "How are we going to do this? What a mess."

"What do you mean? A mess?" she asked.

"Well, to be honest, you don't like me ... and I don't trust you, so how are we going to work together?"

Lissy stood up so suddenly her chair tipped over behind her and hit the floor with a crash. She strode around her desk.

"You don't trust me," she said with a strange look on her face. He looked up at her.

"Did you say, you don't trust me?" she repeated, her voice getting louder. She pushed his shoulders and he had to balance to stop the chair from tipping back.

"Let me tell you something, Mr. High and Mighty Professor, Mr. Spoiled and Idolised Big Brother, Mr. Just Drifting around the Pacific Liar! You're the one who can't be trusted. I am sick of your 'holier than thou' attitude. You want to lay all the ground rules? Well, now I'll tell you how we'll work together. You will show me some respect, you will develop some integrity, and you will not tell me what to do with my life. Is that clear?"

He looked up at her, eyes flashing and that wonderful hair, falling from that ridiculous clip. He reached up and pulled the clip from her hair, studying her as her eyes widened. She backed away from him until she was against the door. He stood up and walked over to her, watching the wary expression on her face.

The anger died.

Aggression slid into desire.

His stance changed, and he broke eye contact to lean forward and slide his lips down her bare neck. His lips paused just below her ear and he felt her shiver.

She turned her head and he found her lips. He was not touching her with any other part of his body; his palms were braced against the door above her head. In her heels, she was almost as tall as he was, and he only had to dip his head slightly to taste her sweet lips.

Soft and willing lips opened beneath his; she

closed her eyes as she gave in to him. His tongue danced with hers, and then he moved his lips to feather soft kisses across her cheeks and slide down her neck once more. He felt her trembling. He paused and placed his forehead against hers.

"Oh, God. I'm like a fourteen-year old boy around you."

"How about we go somewhere public and lay down some ground rules for work and home?" Her voice was husky.

"One more kiss," he said pulling her into him. He could not believe the effect she had on him. The hard part was, despite his inability to resist her, he knew that he couldn't trust her. He was sure she was playing head games with both he and Tom.

He pulled out of the kiss with a groan, ran his hand through his cropped hair and looked at her, feeling disgusted with his behaviour.

"Cafeteria, five minutes." He walked out and pulled the door shut firmly behind him.

Chapter Nine

It took fifteen minutes before Melissa was composed enough to go to the food court. She stood at the door of the cafeteria. Nick was sitting reading the paper, with a mug of coffee in front of him. The cafeteria was crowded and noisy and that was just how she liked it for this meeting. She went to the counter, ordered her coffee and moved across to join him at the table.

"Thank you for meeting with me, Dr. McIntyre." His voice was calm, without a trace of emotion, and she nodded in return.

"What I would like to do is discuss our research and how we are going to work together. We are both mature adults and professionals and know that we have some personal issues. However, you'll agree that we must work around this to get the research report completed. You're aiming for your associate professorial promotion and I want to finish my thesis. This research is critical for both of us. Do you agree?"

She nodded. This formal Nick was easier to

deal with than the man who'd just kissed her senseless in her office. Her face heated, and she swallowed, focusing on what he was saying.

"What I propose is that once we're finished at the end of semester, I'll return to the Pacific and continue my studies in the field, and we will not have to spend any more time together."

She looked at him, trying to imagine not seeing him.

"Well?" he asked. "Do you have an opinion on that?"

She certainly did. The thought of not seeing him again tore at her heartstrings, but there was no way she was going to share that with him.

"That sounds like a good plan, Professor. I also think that a lot of our collaboration can be done by email, and we shouldn't need to meet more than once a week to discuss our progress in person. Do you agree with that?"

He nodded. She drained her coffee cup, stood up, and left him to his paper and coffee.

Melissa returned to her office and decided to leave early and work from home. After she cleared her mail, emailed some files to herself and set her laptop to auto reply, she walked past Jenny's office and put her hand in the door.

"Hey, Jen. I have decided to take a half day of time in lieu, to get myself organised. I'm going to be snowed under with the new project and I need some personal time."

Jen looked at her with concern.

"Are you feeling okay? You're very flushed."

"Just a head cold coming on, back in the air conditioning always does it. I'll see you in the morning."

She took the long route home and pulled up at the lookout on the edge of town. She stood at the brass compass plate that pointed in all directions to many locations and traced her finger over the arrow that pointed east and said Coffs Harbour, 118 miles. Looking east, she saw paddocks of brown grass burned by the early frosts of winter, dotted with sheep, very different to the verdant green of the coast and even further away from the sapphire vista of the Islands that were embedded in her heart.

Not only did the pictures of the boat and islands flash through her head, but a tanned sailor with a bandana around his head, singing a silly song to her filled her thoughts. The same sailor who had taken her to places she had never been before, in an unforgettable night of passion. She stood looking towards the east for a long time. If only Gramps was still alive. She had some big life decisions to make. A solitary tear spilled over her cheek and she brushed it away. Looking around, she saw that she was alone.

Okay, girl, let it all out, and then apply some

analytical methods to this problem. She put her hand down on her arms and let the tears fall.

She blew her nose, climbed back into her car, and turned the car towards home, putting in her favourite mix CD, sang along, and felt much better when she turned into the driveway. Mrs. Mac was in her garden as usual, and she looked up with a worried expression on her face. She took one look at Lissy's red eyes and stood with her hands on her ample hips. She wagged her finger at her as she opened the car door.

"I knew something was wrong when that man turned up on Saturday. Then you were bunkered down in your cottage all weekend. Come on, we're going to have some lunch and a nice cup of tea, and you can tell me all about it."

Taking Melissa's hand, she led her across the driveway, through her wild cottage garden and up the steps into a warm welcoming kitchen. Soup bubbled on the old combustion stove and the smell of baking bread made her mouth water.

"Mrs. Mac, you're a sweetheart," she said, pulling out a kitchen chair and sitting at the pine table in the middle of the kitchen. Her elderly landlady bustled around and made a pot of tea, covering it with a knitted tea cosy with pink tassels hanging down the sides.

She poured a cup, and handed Melissa a piece of warm bread, dripping with butter. "Soup's nearly ready."

"I'll have to go for an extra-long walk now!" Melissa said with a chuckle.

"Now," said Mrs. Mac. "What were all these tears about?"

She took a sip of her tea and thought about how much to tell Mrs. Mac. She had to be careful. Armidale was a small city and the Richards family were well known. She also had to think of Nick's reputation, as well as her own. On the other hand, she knew she could trust Mrs. Mac. She was a kind friend who had supported her since she had moved into town two years ago, not knowing a soul. Mrs. Mac sat down at the table and reached across for her hands and rubbed her fingers.

"It's okay, you don't have to tell me. I know it has to do with that man. Never trust a man on a motorbike. They were always my undoing when I was young!" Mrs. Mac winked and giggled.

She smiled. "Mrs. Mac, you are naughty. I know you're just saying that to make me feel better." Taking a deep breath, she outlined her dilemma in simple terms.

"I have some important decisions to make and I decided to come home and apply some of my research methodology to the problem, without interruption. I really miss Gramps. He was always my sounding board." Mrs. Mac raised an eyebrow at Melissa, indicating that she understood what she really wanted was to get away from the professor for some thinking time.

"Gramps told me to follow my destiny before he died. He didn't approve of my thoughts on love and marriage."

"What do you mean?"

"Well, Mum's been married four times, and she always falls in love and says that she has found the 'one.' I was lucky when she married Greg McIntyre, because he provided such a stable background for me through my teens. But Greg was too busy working and Mum got bored, and she met Lincoln at one of her courses and divorced Greg."

She paused and took a sip of her tea.

"I stayed on at boarding school and Greg paid for me to finish my schooling and helped me with my university costs. I lost touch with him when he remarried, but I've kept his name because he was the only father I ever really had."

"So your Mum is with Lincoln now?" Mrs. Mac asked.

Lissy gave a rueful sigh.

"No. Now Mum is with Lars. The new 'the one' and I'm waiting to see how long that lasts. Although Gramps reckoned he was the one this time. So you can see why I don't believe in romantic love."

Mrs. Mac shook her head. "You mustn't let your mother's experiences taint your view on life and love."

"That's what Gramps always said. Now I have a lovely friend who said he was thinking about proposing to me. I like him very much, and I trust that he wouldn't let me down. I think maybe we *could* have a good life together."

She reached for another piece of bread and paused as she lathered it with butter.

"Then there's the motorbike professor—my new neighbour. We have this explosive effect on each other; however, I don't like the man. He's untrustworthy and he has no integrity. Now I have to work with him and try to fight my attraction for him, and to top it all off, I live next door to him."

Mrs. Mac shook her head. "Oh dear. You can't do an empirical analysis of this one. I would be like your Gramps and tell you not to rush into a convenient relationship just because you don't think you believe in love. You're the only one who can truly know what's best for you." A little smile played around her mouth. "But, I am the landlady and I can evict any tenant. Especially if he is hassling my *favourite* tenant."

"Oh no, Mrs. Mac, you can't do that, I wouldn't expect that. I'm going to think about what Tom said...'

"Tom? Not Tom Richards who picked you up the other night? But isn't he Nick's brother. They're a lovely family ... and then there was

Olivia. Oh, dear girl. You poor thing. You do have some serious decisions to make, don't you?"

Melissa gently pulled her hands from Mrs. Mac's tight grip and stood. The old lady bustled over to the stove, served out another bowl of soup and insisted she take it home.

"I'm a big girl now and there's an associate professorship that I really want, no matter who I have to work with. Thanks for the soup, and don't worry about me. I'll be better in no time."

And I will, she thought as she walked slowly back to her flat.

Even though she couldn't help listening for the sound of a motorbike coming up the road.

Chapter Ten

Lissy was pleased with the composure and professionalism she maintained for the rest of the week. She survived three meetings with Nick in the first week they worked together. As she became absorbed in his research, she realised there were many similarities in the viewpoints they had been exploring. In his office one day late in the week, she said, "Nick, the parallels in our research documents are remarkable. My research from the primary sources, and your first-hand research and the oral histories you've recorded in the Cook Islands, indicate almost the same pattern of Polynesian migration."

"The only place our research differs is the date of the first migration to New Zealand. The Cook Islanders are convinced that the great Maori migrations to New Zealand began from Rarotonga possibly as early as the fifth century AD. Current thought is that the starting point was Ngatangiia on the eastern side of Rarotonga. There's a gap in the fringing reef at the widest part of the island's lagoon."

Nick looked across at her. "I'm going to have to make one more trip out to record the last hereditary chief before I can finalise my report. I'd like you to come with me."

Lissy raised her head and looked directly at him, her heart thudding slow and heavy.

"Come with you?"

He put his hands up. "No hidden agenda, I promise. I'd like you to see the research happening firsthand. It'll help you write the report. I would invite whoever was working with me on the same trip, even if it wasn't you. We're professionals and we can be cool about this, can't we?"

She continued to look at him as thoughts raced through her head. She looked back down at her work. "I'd look forward to that, Professor. I haven't done much work in the field lately."

She thought about how far they'd come this week. A common interest in the research had made them put their personal differences aside. What Nick didn't know, and never would if she had anything to do with it, was how difficult the week had been for her. How did a woman ignore a man, who could make her respond with a look, an accidental brushing of hands, or even the sound of his voice at the end of the telephone? She was even a shaking mess when she saw an email pop up from him!

The phone on Nick's desk rang and after greeting the caller briefly, he held the phone out to her.

"It's Tomas, for you," he said tersely. She raised her eyebrows, surprised at his curt tone.

"Hello, Tom," she said guardedly. Nick sat there and watched her as she spoke to his brother, his arms folded across his chest. She turned her back to him.

"Yes, I'm fine, thank you." She paused, listening to Tom. "Yes, we've been busy, it's a very tight time frame until the report is due."

She glanced over her shoulder at Nick; he was staring at her with his lips set in a straight line. She ignored him and focused on the call.

"Lunch, tomorrow, that would be great. See you at 12:30. Bye."

Gently placing the telephone on the desk in its cradle, she turned to Nick and put her hands on her hips. "What exactly is the matter with you now, Professor Richards?"

He continued to look at her without saying a word. He stood slowly and walked over to the desk and took her elbows in his hands, keeping a distance between them. It was the first time he had deliberately touched her in a week and she felt her heart rate escalate as a warm tingling shot up her arms. Pulling away from his grip, she tossed her head angrily, and the usual recalcitrant curls fell out of her clip. He reached up and tucked the stray curl behind her ear, and a shiver ran down her back as Nick's fingers brushed her neck.

"If I asked you reasonably and seriously not to see my brother, what would you say?"

"I would ask why." She turned her face away from him and closed her eyes, shutting him out before he could see past her expression of indifference. All she really wanted was to reach out and touch him. Turning back to him, she looked up into a granite-like visage.

She was wearing flat pumps today and had to lean back a little to see his eyes. As she stepped away, he reached for her again and pulled her close. Lowering his head, he moved his face so close to hers she could feel his breath on her skin.

"My brother's an easy target," he said. "He was hurt badly by his last girlfriend, and he's always had this life plan mapped out. We all tease him about it, but I know he's serious about being married and settled by thirty-five. Somehow, you've gotten into his good graces and I think he's starting to look at you with a view to marriage. I want to warn you, before he springs it on you. You need to stop leading him on, before it's too late."

Once again, Lissy could feel the slow burn of anger that Nick always seemed to light in her, starting in the pit of her stomach and working its way up to heat her cheeks. She pulled her arms from his and stepped away from him.

"And what if I was to tell you that it's too late, we've already discussed it, and I'm seriously considering it?"

His face darkened. He spoke slowly and enunciated each word clearly, locking his gaze with hers and holding her elbows firmly in a tight grip.

"I would tell you that I would stop it in any way I could... whatever it took."

"Whatever it took?" Her voice was ice-cold. "That sounds like a threat. I'm sick to death of your attitude. You treat me as though I'm a total gold-digger, with no morals and certainly no feelings. Obviously, in your mind, I'm not good enough for the hallowed Richards family." She took a deep breath and poked a finger into his chest.

"Let me remind you, *you* slept with *me* on the Islands too."

She turned away from him in disgust, letting her breath out slowly. "I've done enough work with you today. I think I'll be sick if I have to spend another moment listening to your holiness. What's it like to be perfect, Nick?"

She picked up her laptop and strode to the door. "I'm going to work in my office. I have enough to work on until next week. Please don't bother me unless it's urgent."

She opened the door and turned to him. "And if it *is* urgent, email me."

She made it back to her office before she lost her temper completely. She flicked the lock on her office door and, with shaking hands, put her little kettle on and made herself a cup of tea.

It's an improvement on the tears anyway.

She was trying to figure out why their holiday relationship had made him so bitter. She recalled the evening they'd had in the restaurant on the island, and the rapport that had developed between them. Although neither of them had been honest about their backgrounds, it had still been an enjoyable evening that had culminated in the most unforgettable night of her life.

Admit it. You would love to be with him again.

She almost dropped her teacup as she realised what had just gone through her mind.

You are falling for the man. Just like your mother, a sucker for looks and charm... although he has been a bit light in the charm department lately.

She put her teacup on the saucer, walked over to the window and looked down at the sweeping lawns of the university. It was lunchtime, and everywhere she looked, there were couples entwined on the grass and walking hand-in-hand.

***

Nick was angry at himself. He already regretted showing his hand to Lissy and asking that she not see Tom anymore. He walked into his office and shut the door firmly, pulling his tie off and throwing it onto the desk.

He sat in his swivel chair and placed his feet on the deeply varnished desk. He hated these stints at the university and the complication of this one in particular, with Lissy's involvement doing his head in. He was much more comfortable out in the Islands in shorts and bare feet, heading out for a surf when the day's work was done.

Even my demeanour changes when I'm in this work situation. If only Tom hadn't called when I was there, I wouldn't have even brought it up.

Shaking his head, he reached over and booted up his laptop, ready to start work and hoping to get it done sooner so he could get the hell away from the university.

And a beautiful red-haired woman who had bewitched him.

Chapter Eleven

The next day Melissa met Tom for lunch. He greeted her in the foyer, reached over, and kissed her cheek, taking her hand to lead her into the restaurant where there were small intimate tables covered with white linen tablecloths. Gleaming cutlery sat on the table and a black-suited waiter was waiting to seat them.

"I've never been in here before. I usually grab a sandwich at the student union," she said looking around, taken aback by the opulence of the staff restaurant.

He smiled at her. "This is where all the high-powered decisions and finances of the university take place. Business lunches with a very good wine list. Would you like wine with your lunch?"

"No, thank you, I have a lot of work to finish this afternoon. I'd fall asleep at my desk," she said laughing.

"How are you finding working with Nick? He can be a hard taskmaster."

Melissa held back all the words that came to

mind, and none were as kind as 'hard taskmaster'. She pulled out her most professional response.

"It's extremely challenging, but I'm learning so much. He has wide experience in the field."

Tom reached over and put his hand on hers.

Lissy looked down and realised that she had absolutely no reaction to his touch. No matter that he was a nice guy who was being very sweet and showing an interest in a relationship with her. She felt more reaction when she turned the hot water tap on, she thought sadly.

"You look tired." Tom looked concerned. "I hope you haven't been losing sleep over what I said the other night. I still think it's not a bad idea."

She looked across the table at him. His white shirt and subtle tie complemented his dark blue suit. His hair was immaculate and his grooming impeccable.

"We're friends, Tom. Let's keep it that way," she said gently.

As she spoke, Nick's strong face intruded on her thoughts, and she pushed him out of her mind. The fact that he had asked her to stop seeing his brother wasn't the reason she was refusing to consider Tom's 'proposition'.

His face fell. "I knew you were going to say that, but you're right. Friends is what we are. While I am thinking of it, I'll have to cancel our usual Friday night this week. A small family occasion has come up."

She nodded at him.

"Not a problem. I've been invited to Clare's thirtieth birthday dinner on Friday night, so that works out well."

He looked relieved and passed her the menu. "However, my mother did ask me to invite you to a barbeque on Saturday afternoon at the farm, if you're free."

Well, that would be one way to annoy Nick, she thought.

"That would be great," she said. "I'm free on Saturday. Is there anything I can bring?"

"No, just yourself. I'll pick you up at about one."

After they finished lunch, Tom insisted on walking her back to her office, even though he was located at the other side of the university in the main administration building. As they walked along the corridor of the history faculty, they heard laughter coming from the staff room. An attractive blonde woman came out of the room, saying over her shoulder, "Professor Richards, you're incorrigible."

Tom rolled his eyes. "Looks like my brother is up to his old tricks with the ladies," he groaned.

Nick was at the door when they passed and looked pointedly at Tom holding Melissa's arm.

Lissy shivered at the angry look he directed

at her as she walked past him.

***

Oddly enough, as the days passed, Nick helped Lissy in her resolve to have as little to do with him as possible. He flew to Sydney twice for meetings and had one overnight visit to Brisbane. He rarely entered her office and only attended a couple of the faculty meetings. He was charming and polite and might as well have been a chance acquaintance. She managed to sit at the other end of the conference table and focus on her laptop on the occasions that he spoke to the faculty.

Contact between them was mostly by email. Nick would send her an area of research that he required her to verify, and she would email the results of her inquiries back to him. As the week drew to a close and he wasn't required for lectures, he worked from home and she didn't even see him at the university.

But it wasn't as easy as she had anticipated to push Nick from her thoughts. She could hear every move he made in the cottage next door and there were times when her resolve was threatened. She heard his shower running, she knew when he had the television on, and she could hear his telephone ring. She felt as though they were living in the same house. She dreamed about him regularly and woke aching, unfulfilled.

Jenny had offered to pick Lissy up at her

place and drive her to Ivy Cottage for Clare's birthday party, and Lissy gladly accepted the offer. She was looking forward to going out to the restaurant with the girls, having a few drinks and forgetting about Nick Richards for one night.

"Wow, look at you! I nearly didn't recognise you. You should wear your hair down more often. You look fantastic!" Jenny said when she laid eyes on Lissy.

She had settled on a brightly patterned skirt that brushed her ankles and a figure-hugging red body suit with a deep-scooped neck. The shell necklace Gramps had given her for her last birthday highlighted a hint of cleavage. She put some mousse in her hair and scrunched her curls, and heavy dangling earrings completed the gypsy look.

"The only downside of being pregnant," Jenny said with a sigh, "is I can't have a drink with the girls tonight."

When they entered Ivy Cottage, they heard a scream of delight as Clare spotted them in the foyer. She came running over with a glass of champagne sloshing in her hand.

"Well, looks like the party has started," said Jenny, leaning over and giving Clare a birthday kiss, narrowly avoiding champagne spilling down her back as Clare returned the hug one-armed.

"Happy Birthday, Clare." Lissy gave her friend a hug before they made their way over to a table, where about twenty of Clare's friends were already seated. Clare made Lissy and Jenny stand up at the end of the table while she introduced them to the other girls. There were a dozen of her friends from school, and others up from Sydney. Clare sounded as though she had already downed a few birthday drinks.

"Ladies, ladies, listen up. These—" she paused and put an arm around Melissa and Jenny, "—are my two very best work friends in the whole, wide world. This is Jenny, and this is Lissy." A chorus of greetings came from the group as Lissy and Jenny sat on the last two vacant chairs.

Lissy looked around the restaurant and was pleased to see only a couple of other tables with customers who were almost finished with their meals. She had a feeling this was going to be a loud and noisy party, quite different from the usually formal Friday night atmosphere at Ivy Cottage. A loud pop signalled the opening of the next bottle of champagne and she took a sip from the glass that was handed to her.

"Happy birthday, Clare," the girls said in a toast, holding up their glasses.

Melissa sat at the side of the table against the wall, and the girl on her left started up a conversation. Within five minutes, she had heard all about the girl's job, her family, and her two broken relationships and how horrible all men were. She didn't get a chance to get a word in and smiled gratefully when Jenny interrupted and rescued her. The waitress came out with menus and the table quietened as the girls discussed what they were going to order.

All of a sudden, Clare hissed across the table at Jenny and Lissy.

"Sssh, sssh. Girls, girls, quick." She was gesturing madly at the door behind them and her whisper was loud enough to be heard by all of the diners in the room.

"It's Johnny Depp," she whispered urgently, pretending to swoon.

Melissa's stomach took a dive to her toes. Refusing to turn around, she waited until the group walked past the table of girls and were seated in the opposite corner of the room. Looking up slowly, she met Nick's sardonic gaze and to her absolute horror, she realised that Nick, Tom, and two very attractive women were seated at the table. From a distance, she heard Clare's voice.

"Earth to Melissa, earth to Melissa." She looked up and saw the waitress standing next to her, pen poised waiting to take her order.

"Oh, sorry." She grabbed the menu in front of her and read out the first thing she saw.

"I'll have the chicken, please."

"Salad and chips, or vegetables?" asked the waitress.

"Ah...salad, please." Her hands were shaking, her heart thudding. She picked up her champagne and drained the glass in one gulp.

Not only was Nick flaunting his next conquest in public, but dependable, honest Tom had a woman with him as well.

"Lissy, are you feeling okay? You're really flushed," said Jenny.

She pulled herself together and plastered a smile on her face. "No, I'm fine. I just need another drink." Grabbing the champagne bottle out of the ice bucket, she filled her glass and tipped her head back and drained the glass in one go.

Clare burst out laughing. "Go, Melissa! This is going to be a great party."

The noise level in the restaurant increased as three more tables filled with customers. Luckily for Melissa, the lights were dim, the girls' table was in a corner, and she could avoid looking at the group of four across the room. On the odd occasion that she glanced over there, Nick was watching her with a tight expression on his face.

Damn him, she thought, and threw back another glass of champagne.

Their group got louder and more raucous as the drinks flowed. Melissa was not used to being out with a group of women determined to let their hair down. Her social life during university had been limited because she had studied hard, determined to succeed.

After a couple more drinks, she stood and announced loudly to the group that she was going to the ladies room and invited all of them to join her. Clare elbowed Jen and said with a giggle, "You'd better go with her, Jen, and make sure she comes back."

As they passed the Richards' table on their way to the restroom, Lissy was pleased to see the shock on Tom's face when he looked up and saw her sashaying past. She waggled her fingers at them.

"Hi, Tom. Hi, Nicky. Hi, lucky ladies with Tom and Nicky" A giggly champagne--fuelled hiccough escaped her lips and Jenny dragged her into the rest room.

"Melissa!" exclaimed Jenny. "The professor is a hunk. Tell me all...you called him by his first name. Have you been out with him or do you just know him from work?"

"Nuh, juss from work", slurred Lissy. "He's a nightmare to work with, very full of himself...not very nice at all."

"What about Tom? Are you still going out with him?"

"Nuh, jush friends. Thought he was different, but they are tarred with the same hairbrush."

Jenny burst out laughing. "Oh, you are so funny with a few drinks under your belt. You mean brush, not hairbrush!"

She tried to be serious for a minute and had to hang on tightly to the basin to keep her balance. She squinted into the mirror and frowned; her curls were out of control.

"Woo...a bit giddy," she announced. "And I'm hungry."

Jenny pulled a chair over and sat her down in front of the mirror. "Okay, let's fix you up a bit." She stood behind Lissy and tried to tame her curls down with her hand. "Speaking of hairbrushes, did you bring yours, hon?"

Lissy fumbled in her bag and tipped it out onto the bench. The contents of the bag rolled around and fell over the edge, just as the two glamorous women who were with Tom and Nick entered the restroom. She dived to the floor to catch lipstick, brushes, keys, and coins as they hit the floor.

"Oh, hello," she said looking up from where she was crouched on the tiles. "Your legs match the rest of you."

The two women laughed and moved into the cubicles.

"Come on," Jenny said. "Our meals will be there soon."

She helped Lissy pick up the contents of her bag, straighten her hair and lipstick, and they headed back into the restaurant after visiting the cubicle.

"Oh, no you don't," said Jenny as Lissy spotted the two empty chairs at the Richards' table and dragged Jenny over. She plonked herself down next to Tom, whose eyes were like saucers.

Nick sat back and folded his arms, looking at them with interest.

"Hi, boys. I would like you to meet my very best friend, Jenny. It's her birthday and she would love a birthday kiss." Another hiccough escaped her red-painted lips and she giggled.

"Hap...happy birthday, Jenny. Nice to meet you," said Tom.

Nick continued to sit and look without speaking, but Melissa caught his eye. She leaned over and said, "Nicky darling, why do you look like the cat that got the cream?"

He shrugged. "I wasn't aware that I did."

Melissa leaned closer; she was sure there was a hint of a smile on those gorgeous lips.

"No." She shook her head and muttered. "Not gorgeous. Not at all"

"Thank you, Tom, but it's actually Clare's birthday," Jenny said. "Come on, Lissy, our meals will be there. See you later."

She grabbed Melissa and pulled her to her feet.

"Come on, we'll leave this pair to their floozies," Melissa said.

Jenny looked mortified and whispered behind her hand to Nick and Tom.

"Sorry, guys. Melissa's had a bit too much champagne."

Jenny dragged her across the restaurant to their table and sat her down next to Clare so that her back was to the Richards' table. She had a whispered conversation with Clare who turned to Lissy and started up a conversation with her.

"So, tell us about your holiday."

Melissa's laugh was shrill, and heads turned at some of the tables close by.

"Ooh..." she giggled. "I had the best time. I went on a yacht and I met a gorgeous man and we..." She was sober enough to think before she continued. "And we became very, very good friends. She paused for a moment. "But now I am home in the cold weather and back at work and the man is horrible."

She stopped and put her head down as the table wavered in front of her. Their meals arrived and she decided she had better eat something. Picking up her knife and fork, she tried to concentrate on her meal, which seemed to be moving from left to right. As she speared a chip, it shot over the table.

Jen leaned over and laughed. "Let me be mum. I'll cut it up for you."

"Nuh. It's easier if I have champagne for

dinner." She picked up her glass and swallowed the rest of her drink on one hit.

After a couple of hours of laughter, conversation, and several more bottles of champagne, Clare decided it was time to go dancing. The other girls had drunk champagne all night and Lissy's out-of-character behaviour didn't stand out too much.

"Who's up for the nightclub?" asked Clare, as they stood in the foyer paying the bill.

The Seven Brothers dance club was around the corner on the next street. Jenny looked tired. "No, but thanks. I think I'm done," she said, as she patted her baby bulge. "Lissy, do you want a ride home now or will you catch a taxi?"

There was movement behind them; Nick was standing in the foyer next to them.

"It's okay, Jenny. I'll take Melissa home. We live close to each other," he said.

Lissy looked up at him and giggled.

"But, Nick, that's not in the rules anywhere, is it? And I want to go dancing."

He shrugged. "I can wait."

"But what about your guests?" Jenny asked.

"Not a problem. Tom will drive the girls back to the farm."

Lissy was faintly aware that there was something bothering her but couldn't put her finger on it. She looked up at him, squinting, trying to figure it out.

"Okay, come on. Nick, you're welcome to come dancing with us," Clare said.

Nick followed them down the steps. As soon as the fresh air hit her, Lissy's head started to swim and her knees buckled.

"Woo..." she said, clutching for the railing.

Strong arms reached beneath her legs as Nick swept her up. The girls were halfway along the street and turned to see if she was all right.

"It's okay, ladies. Melissa has decided she wants to go home now." Nick reassured them. She squinted again, looking up at him, trying to figure out who he was and what he was doing, but it was all too hard.

"Night, girls," she muttered putting her head on the lovely warm, soft shoulder that was beneath her head. She recognised the familiar smell of spicy aftershave and snuggled in closer. She was vaguely aware of being bundled into a cold car and having her skirt tucked in around her.

She slipped into the realms of a very drunken sleep.

Chapter Twelve

The screeching birds outside the window woke Melissa at dawn. Opening one eye, she tried to ignore the little hammers that were tapping in her head. Her mouth was so dry it felt as though her tongue was sticking to its roof. Looking around, she recognised her room and squinted, trying to figure out why it was facing the wrong way—the window was in the wrong place and the door was facing east. The colours were right, but her furniture was gone. It was like a parallel universe. The bed moved, and she reached out her hand to stop the head spin and pulled her hand back as she unexpectedly encountered a warm, bare chest.

She opened her other eye and grimaced as the bright morning sun streaming in the window bathed the tanned body next to her in sunlight. Nick was flat on his back, a sheet covering him from the waist down. She closed her eyes, hoping it was a hallucination caused by her hangover. Opening her eyes again, she looked down at herself and groaned–she was wearing an unfamiliar shirt and her underwear. Sexy, red lace underwear that she had put on under her gypsy skirt last night. She groaned again and tried to sit up but fell back to the pillow as the room began to spin. The bed shook as Nick's deep laugh made her head ache even more.

"What are you doing in my bed?" she croaked. Her voice sounded like dry sandpaper rasping on a board.

"No, what are you doing in my bed?" Awareness dawned as she looked around.

"Oh, God," she groaned, "what have you done?"

She sat up, clutching the shirt across her breasts and tried to swing her legs over the side of the bed. His shoulders shook with laughter. She could not hold her head, keep her balance and clutch his shirt together at the same time.

"Lissy," he laughed. "I haven't done anything. You did it all by yourself."

She managed to sit up and leaned back against the pillows, both hands over her eyes.

"How did I get home?"

"I carried you."

"What, from the restaurant?"

"No, to my car. Unfortunately, you were sick on the way home and when you couldn't find your key, it was easier to bring you in here, rather than wake Mrs. Mac up for the spare key."

She moaned again through her hands, unsure

if it was the distress of finding herself in his bed, or the hangover causing it. "Let me die, now."

"Would you like a cup of tea, Lissy?" He'd managed to contain his laughter, but now he was grinning down at her. She felt so ill, she couldn't even appreciate the bare chest in her vision. The way she was feeling, she didn't think she'd ever appreciate anything again.

"Yes, please, and aspirin," she said, rolling over, pulling the sheet up over her head, and promptly went back to sleep.

Melissa woke up the second time to an empty cottage, and a cold cup of tea on the bedside table. She sat up and gulped down the aspirin Nick had left her. Lying back down, she thought about the night before, and dread washed over her as she remembered some of the evening.

A family function indeed. She thought about the two stunning women who had been with Nick and Tom last night. With black cascading curls down their backs and dressed in elegant clothes, they both could have been models. Something Nick had said last night tugged at her memory, but she couldn't hold on to the thought as her head spun.

As the thoughts ran through her aching head, she put both hands over her face and groaned.

Nature called, and she swung her legs over the side of the bed. At least Nick had had the decency to leave her alone in his bed. When she stood, the room spun; she squinted at the bedside clock and was shocked to see it was after noon. She stumbled into Nick's bathroom and tripped over her skirt and top on the floor. She almost passed out with embarrassment. There was no way she could ever look him in the eye again.

Let alone work with the man.

But you have to, reminded her ambitious side, *if you want that associate professorship.*

She looked into the mirror in his bathroom and sighed. Her mascara had run down one cheek, surrounded by the worst case of bed hair she had ever seen. The other cheek was a map of pillow wrinkles and she hoped Nick hadn't looked too closely when he had left her the tea and the aspirin. Scrubbing her face and loosely tying back her hair, Melissa repaired the damage as best she could. Gathering her clothes from the floor, she turned her nose up at the smell of vomit. The next problem was finding her keys and getting into her side of the cottage without being seen. She sat down on the bed and pulled her cell phone out of her bag. At least that was still there. She dialled Mrs. Mac's number. It was going to be difficult explaining why she needed the spare key. The phone rang, but there wasn't an answer. She felt relieved; no explanations needed as to why she was semi-naked in Nick's cottage without her key.

She had no idea where Nick had gone or how long he would be. She had to get out of here, and into her own flat before he got back. Looking around, she spotted her shoes underneath the table. Gathering her clothes, shoes and bag under one arm, she crept over to the door.

If I go around the back, I can get into the laundry window.

Lissy looked down to make sure she was decent, and decided that the long, white shirt covered enough. Opening the front door, she stepped out and peered around the corner. Nick's car was in the driveway, but there was no sign of him. She pulled the front door shut behind her and then groaned; she shouldn't have, in case she couldn't get in her window. She tiptoed around the veranda, keeping an eye out for neighbours, but there was not a soul in sight. The veranda tiles were cold under her bare feet and she walked around the corner towards her back door. As she crept around to the back of the house, she was horrified to hear another car pull up in the driveway. Doors slammed, and she looked around in vain, knowing there was nowhere to hide on her porch. Footsteps crunched on the gravel around the side of the house, and she prayed for the ground to open up as not only Nick, but Tom, walked around to the back steps.

"Melissa, I er...I'm here to pick you up for

the barbeque," Tom said.

She looked angrily from one to the other. Nick held up a shopping bag. "I was walking back from the shops, and Tom stopped and picked me up. Chips and coke... good hangover food." He had a smug grin on his face.

Tom looked from one to the other in confusion, and then his face changed as he realised she was wearing Nick's shirt and not a lot under it.

"Lissy?" He turned to his brother, confusion written all over his face. "Nick?"

Melissa snapped back. "It isn't what it looks like. Anyway, who were those women *you* were out with last night?"

"They were family," Nick said. "Mama asked Tom and me to take two cousins visiting from Italy out for dinner since she and Dad had a function to attend. Isabella and Talia were most amused that some little hussy thought we were their boyfriends."

She looked at him open-mouthed. "You set this whole thing up, didn't you?"

"Set what up?" Tom asked again, stepping forward.

"Help me get into my cottage please," she said stonily. "Nick can explain it all to you later. The laundry window should be open. If you push it right up, you should be able to climb in, Nick, and open the door for me."

She sat down on the chair at her back door and folded her arms. Tom looked at her with a strange look on his face but didn't speak. Nick handed her the bag of groceries as he strolled past. He pushed up the laundry window with some difficulty and climbed through the small space. Tom still looked as though he was in shock. She obviously wasn't in contention for wife of the future anymore. *Good.* At least Tom could forget about his stupid idea.

"Am I right in thinking that you're not coming out to the farm for lunch?" asked Tom.

She responded by crossing her arms tightly and trying to look dignified—as dignified as one could look in a man's shirt, with bed hair and bare feet.

"No, thank you, Tom. I will not be coming to lunch. Please thank your mother though."

"Right then," he said, pulling himself together. "I'll call you later." He looked so confused, for a moment she felt sorry for him, but she was feeling too sick and frustrated to explain everything to him.

Nick can do it later.

Tom disappeared down the stairs and his car started up and went down the driveway.

Her back door opened, and Nick came out and stood in front of her. He held out his hand to help her up. Ignoring it, she leaned down and picked up her clothes and shoes from the floor, leaving the bag of groceries behind. She stood up and walked into her cottage.

"Thank you for bringing me home safely last night and thank you for the bed and the aspirin." She turned to close the door but looked down as a large booted foot stopped it from closing.

***

"Wait. You and I have some talking to do." Nick pushed his way past her, groceries in hand and the door behind him. He went over to the table and pulled out a chair and sat down, leaning back in the chair, his boots crossed casually in front of him. He looked settled in for a long chat.

Melissa dropped her clothes and shoes and groaned with her hands over her face. "Why has my life turned upside down since I met you.?" She looked down at him, shaking her head, and then put a hand to her forehead.

"Headache, still?" Nick pushed the chair back and rose to his feet, her distress tugging at him. He had deliberately taken their cousins to Ivy Cottage last night, knowing that Lissy would be at the birthday party. It had been the talk of the faculty staff room the whole week. He had hoped that she would see Tom with the girls and think the worst. His plan had worked, but he couldn't understand why he felt so bad about it this morning. He shouldn't care about her being upset.

The sight of Lissy in his shirt, legs barely covered by the shirttail, hands over her face, was the last straw. He'd watched her sleep in the early hours this morning, before she had woken up the first time, and the feelings that had settled in his chest were unfamiliar. He couldn't resist her. He was going crazy thinking about her.

Reaching out, he held her shoulders gently.

"What do you think you're doing?" she asked, but there was a tremor in her voice. He took her hands in his and raised one to his mouth, running his lips over the inside of her palm, as he looked down into her eyes. She closed her eyes and swayed, and he reached out and caught her before she fell.

"You're going to be the death of me. God help me, this is all I think about."

He slipped his hands up beneath her shirt, brushing his fingers against her warm skin. She leaned into him, as he placed his hands on her back. He rested his head on top of hers and took comfort from the warmth of her body leaning into his.

"I need a shower and I need to brush my teeth."

Her vulnerability brought that unfamiliar feeling back. Nick lifted her and carried her into the bathroom. Lowering her gently onto the tiled floor, he turned on the shower taps and hot steam billowed out of the shower recess. She rested her forehead against his shoulder. "Thank you. I'll be fine now."

"I'll wait in the bedroom." Nick closed the bathroom door and sat on the bed. He stared at the door, wishing he had stayed in there with her, but it wasn't the right thing to do.

For more than one reason. Not just because she was hung over. His response to Lissy confused him, and he didn't think rationally when he was around her. He sat there brooding for a few minutes, and then looked up when the door opened. Her cheeks had colour in them again, and she had a towel wrapped around her.

"Can you pass my robe please?" Her voice was soft as she stood in the bathroom doorway, one hand against her forehead. Nick stared at her as the unfamiliar feeling intensified. What he wanted most was to make her smile again. Emotion clogged his throat. All of a sudden he wasn't sure whether he could survive this.

"Where is it?" He stood and cleared his throat.

"On the hook on the back of the door."

Walking over to the door, he reached up and lifted the white towelling robe from the hook. The next time she emerged from the bathroom, the robe wrapped tightly around her, her damp hair was combed and pulled back into a clip. Her eyes were shadowed and again, her vulnerability hit him like a sixer.

For the life of him he couldn't help himself.

He moved across to place a gentle kiss on the dark shadows under her eyes. "Late nights don't agree with you," he said softly.

"It's you who doesn't agree with me," she murmured as she leaned into him. "Nick?"

"Yes?" He feathered another kiss across her cheek.

"Why did you set me up last night?"

Nick stepped back and shook his head. "I think you need to get some sleep now. We'll talk about it when you're feeling more human. In fact, we need to talk about a few things."

Chapter Thirteen

Lissy slept the afternoon away and woke after the sun had set. She stretched, and for a moment, she smiled and thought how good she felt, considering the amount she had drunk the night before. The memory of the afternoon slammed into her. She rolled over and groaned, pulling the pillow over her head. She lay there quietly and became aware of the noises coming from the other side of the cottage. Nick was still home and obviously hadn't gone to the barbeque at the farm. She groaned as she thought of the mistake she had made assuming Nick's cousins were their dates, and when she remembered the look on Tom's face that afternoon, she wondered if she would ever be able to face him again.

I need to talk to Nick and find out exactly what he was trying to achieve last night. If I'm going to do it, I'm going to do it now.

She climbed out of bed, had a quick shower to warm up, dressed in tights and a jumper, and ran a brush through her unruly curls. She brushed her teeth, humming to herself. This sexual tension with Nick had finally come to a head, and they would have to sort something out. It didn't have to be a lifelong relationship; maybe they could just see each other for a while, enjoy each other's company and move on. She opened the door to the veranda and Luney shot between her legs, meowing for her dinner.

"Oh, Luney, I'm so sorry. I forgot all about you. You must be starving." She tipped out some food into the dish, closed the door and walked outside. Tapping lightly on Nick's door, she stood, waiting for him to open the door. It seemed to take forever. She heard him moving around the room and knocked a second time. Finally, the door opened, and he looked down at her. His face was impassive, and her stomach dropped.

"You'd better come in."

Oh my God, here we go again. He's so bloody moody. She followed him into his living room.

"Sit down. Would you like a cup of tea, or a drink...?" A ghost of a smile crossed his lips.

"A cup of tea is fine," she said. She sat down at the dining table; he went into the kitchen and filled the kettle. He stayed in the kitchen until it boiled, and she heard him clinking about with the teacups. He placed a neatly set tray with tea, milk and sugar on the table in front of her. Sitting down opposite her, he poured her tea silently. She began to feel anxious, the easy mood that had been there this afternoon had gone. Her confidence was fast disappearing.

Nick sat back and looked at her. "What can I do for you?"

She dug deep for a strength that she did not feel. "I came in to thank you for bringing me home last night and looking after me, and to let you know I'm fully recovered now. I'm going into work tomorrow to catch up, so I won't be around if you're looking for me."

She was babbling, her hands were tingling, her heart thudding and her stomach churning with the rejection she could sense from him, but she was determined not to let him see how upset she was. She drained her tea, smiled brightly at him, and lied.

"Poor Luney is waiting for her tea, so I'll catch you later in the week." Standing, she held her hand out to him. "Friends?"

He slowly took her hand and looked up at her.

"Yes, friends," he replied.

With a smile fixed on her face, her jaw aching from holding it there, she walked to the door and let herself out with a wave over her shoulder.

"See you Monday, maybe."

She just made it to her door and let herself

into her side of the house, before she bent double, the intensity of his rejection hitting her like a physical blow. She sat in her soft lounge chair, arms wrapped around her stomach, and rocked backward and forward.

She wasn't good enough for him.

The hurt went too deep. Luney jumped on the chair, sensing her distress and rubbed Lissy's cheek. She reached down to the floor, pulling the blanket that had fallen up over her and the cat and closed her eyes, willing sleep to take her into oblivion.

She spent the rest of the weekend hiding in her cottage. She was as quiet as a mouse, so Nick would think she had gone out. She could not cope with any questions from Mrs. Mac and she certainly didn't want to see Nick.

Skulking around in my own home, like a prisoner.

The phone rang late on Sunday night. She had pulled on her fluffy flannel pyjamas and sheepskin boots for comfort, and was sitting in front of the fire trying to read some notes in preparation for the following day at work. The delay before the beeps indicated an international call, and shortly after the tone, she heard her mother's voice.

"Hey, darling, just ringing to touch base. I haven't had an email from you for a few days."

"Sorry, Mum, I've been busy at work, and

then I went out with the girls on Friday night and I've spent most of the weekend recovering."

"A big night?" Her mother's voice was playful.

"Yes, most out of character as you know, but a very big night for me. Never again. I still feel tired...I drank way too much champagne."

"Lissy...?"

Here we go, thought Lissy, *the end of Lars. I've been waiting for it.*

She propped her chin in her hand and waited for the news. "Yes, Mum?"

"Lars and I will be arriving in two weeks, a little bit earlier than we planned." Lissy sat up, surprised by the news.

"I know you're busy at work, but would you be able to get away to meet us at the coast?"

"Absolutely. I wouldn't miss it for the world. I'm so looking forward to finally meeting Lars. I can't get leave but I could come down on the Friday night and stay for the weekend. How long are you staying?"

"How about we meet you at Gramps's place and then come back to Armidale with you, so we can have some time with you after you finish work? If you have room for us, I can cook, and Lars can keep the fire going. He's very good at that." Her mother laughed. "And I don't just mean a wood fire. He's a wonderful man. I can't wait for you to meet him."

"That sounds great. It'll be so good to see you. I'm going down to the coast next weekend, so I'll get some supplies in and air out Gramps's cottage."

Her mother hung up after extracting a promise from Lissy to take care of herself and not go drinking again.

By Monday morning, Lissy had shed the hangover and accepted that any chance of a relationship with Nick was not going to happen. She puttered around, getting ready for work. The cottage sparkled, the ironing was done for the week, and she'd cooked dinners ahead and placed them in the freezer.

Still feeling embarrassed, she hoped Nick had not sensed the real reason that she'd gone knocking on his door on Saturday afternoon. She tried to hold on to her anger, but she felt quite sad.

He's impossible to understand.

She groaned as she remembered the look on Tom's face when he had seen her come out of Nick's door, obviously fresh from Nick's bed. She was determined to phone him from her office on Monday and explain that it wasn't what it looked like, not that she owed Tom anything, but they had been friends, and Nick was his brother.

She stood in front of the mirror, putting on her makeup and pinning up her hair.

I hate the way Nick makes me feel.

No, you don't, said the truthful part of her heart. *He makes you feel alive and you love it.*

She paused, mascara wand halfway to the wide eyes staring back at her from the mirror.

Where the hell did that come from?

She was not going to listen to her heart. After the weekend, she realised that she needed to get out of this mess. In a way, she was grateful to him for his clear rejection. Better now than later, when she'd gotten used to having him around. God knows, she had seen the effect of that on her mother over the years.

Lissy finished applying her makeup, all trace of hangovers, tiredness and tears camouflaged. Nodding at her calm reflection, she moved to her bedroom and chose her red suit and highest heels for confidence and headed off to work.

***

"Woohoo, here's Dr. McIntyre, life and soul of the party." Lissy was greeted by giggles from her work colleagues as she walked tough the main office. She'd forgotten about Clare and Jenny, as she had worried all weekend about Nick and Tom.

"Don't know about life and soul, but the headache was a beauty," she said laughing with them, not letting any hint of her true feelings slip.

I could win an Oscar, she thought to herself. It was like being two different people—the happy carefree woman chatting to her friends, with a sad and tightly curled up emotional wreck hidden deep inside.

"Did Professor Richards get you home safely?" Jenny asked.

"Yes, he was very nice. Got me home safely," she said, lying. "I slept most of the weekend away. Nothing like a good night out with the girls to clear the cobwebs."

"Are these yours, Melissa? They found them in the ladies room." Clare held up a set of keys.

"Yes, what a relief," said Lissy. "I was worried they'd been stolen."

"How did you get in on Friday night?" asked Jenny.

"Um, through the window." The vision of Nick climbing through the window, with Tom looking like his world had come to an end as she stood there in Nick's shirt, popped into her head.

"Anyway, girls, I have a ton of work today, so I'll catch you later," she said as she turned towards her office. She entered the room and shut the door firmly, preparing to bunker down. The morning passed uneventfully and there was no sign of Nick.

She called Tom as soon as she sat at her desk. He answered his telephone across the other side of the campus in his usual calm and polite manner.

"Tom, it's Melissa."

"Good morning, Melissa." Tom's voice was guarded.

"I owe you an apology. I was very rude to you and your cousins Friday night."

Tom accepted her apology and said he'd made her excuses at Saturday's lunch. He cleared his throat as she said good-bye to him.

"Err...just one more thing, Melissa."

She held the telephone to her ear, looking out at the clear winter sky through her window, wondering what was coming.

"Yes?"

"Melissa, I think it would be best if we don't have dinner this Friday evening." He said quietly. "I'm not sure what's happening with you and Nick..."

"Nick and I, we're not an item."

He sounded sceptical. "Be warned, while I love Nick dearly as my brother, I am aware he can be hard on women. He has never forgotten how badly Olivia, and then Rebecca, hurt him."

"Tom, I have to go now." She didn't want to hear about Nick's love life.

"Just be careful with Nick, Melissa. He knew you were going to be at Ivy Cottage on Friday night and he insisted we go there. We'd planned on staying at home. He's up to something. I know Nick well and I'd hate to see you get hurt."

She put the phone down carefully, determined not to let thoughts of any scheme of Nick's interfere with her hard-won calm or her work. Booting up her computer, she tried to immerse herself in her work and forget about Nick Richards.

Lissy spent the week in her office, typing up her research and annotating her web references. She survived on cups of coffee and didn't leave her office during the day for the whole week except for the faculty meeting on Thursday. To her great relief, Nick was at a teleconference in another room and the meeting finished before she could attend. She also managed to stagger her work hours, leaving and arriving so that she didn't see Mrs. Mac or Nick. She was feeling so brittle she thought she would snap if anyone tried to have a conversation with her. Sleepless nights and dreams of Nick in her bed contributed to her edginess.

Chapter Fourteen

The week dragged, and it was with a great sense of relief that Lissy turned eastward out of Armidale after work on Friday afternoon. She was headed for Gramps's house on the coast, where she would meet up with Mum and Lars next weekend. When she deposited Luney and Sylvester with her neighbour, Mrs. Mac's brow furrowed.

"I've hardly seen you this week. You've been working too hard," she said. "And you look tired...*and* you've lost weight. Are you eating enough?"

"It's okay, Mrs Mac, work is really busy. That's why I'm taking a break down at the coast this weekend. Catch a bit of sun and warm up." She reached over and hugged her friend. "You really are a sweetie to help with this pair." She handed over the cage, but Mrs. Mac persisted.

"Is that professor still giving you a hard time? I've hardly seen him around either."

"Just at work," said Lissy. "We have a deadline looming." Mrs. Mac still looked sceptical as Lissy backed out of the driveway.

She always enjoyed the drive from Armidale down to the coast. The road wound past the green pastures of the huge cattle properties on the fertile plateau for the first hundred miles, before it meandered through the quaint village of Dorrigo, perched on the edge of the escarpment. A flashing sign at the top of the mountain road advised the roadway would be closed for repair at night from Friday evening through to Sunday.

The drive down from the top of the mountain to the coast through the World Heritage rainforest always made Lissy nervous as the narrow, winding road passed two waterfalls that often crossed the roadway in heavy rain. Crews were constantly repairing the road as the mountain was unstable and there were frequent rock falls. Although the scenery was breathtaking, she breathed a sigh of relief as she reached the bottom of the mountain and turned on to the flat land of the Bellinger River valley.

An hour later, she turned into the driveway of Gramps's fishing cottage behind the dunes of Blackrock Beach. The afternoon light had faded, and the headlights lit the front of the old cottage. The grass was long, and newspapers littered the front porch. Removing the key from under the big rock in the unkempt garden, Lissy squealed when a sticky spider web clung to her face as she crossed the porch. Her footsteps echoed on the wooden floorboards of the front hall and she swallowed a sob, her throat aching, when she saw Gramps's raincoat hanging on the hook inside the front door. The house was silent and cold, and she looked at the mess scattered throughout the small space. Piles of newspapers covered the table and chairs, and boxes of old fishing gear lined the bench along the wall.

Next weekend, when Mum is here...this weekend is to recharge my emotional batteries, not cry over Gramps's belongings. It was late, and she was tired, so after a quick sandwich and a wash, she went to bed in her old room. The gentle lull of the waves breaking on the sand lulled her off to the deepest sleep she'd had all week.

##

The screeching of the rainbow lorikeets woke her the next morning. Lying in bed, Lissy—she always felt like Lissy, not Melissa, when she was at Gramps's place—watched the birds hang upside down in the huge bottlebrush tree outside her window as they ate the honey from the red flowers. Their squawking contrasted with the muted roar of the ocean coming over the dunes. Stretching, she stepped out of bed feeling more at ease than she had for weeks. This was her true home, and the familiar sights, smells and sounds soothed her.

She pulled on a pair of shorts and a T-shirt,

appreciating the warmth of the coast. Even though it was winter, the warmth from the ocean kept the temperature mild all year. Putting some money in her back pocket for breakfast at the cafe on her way home, she headed off for a walk along the beach. Lissy waved at a few familiar faces as she walked to the boat ramp. Recognizing Harvey's battered four-wheel drive and rusted trailer, she realised he was still out fishing for the morning. Crossing the esplanade, she headed up the hill and walked onto the veranda of the coffee shop on the headland overlooking the beach. She would sit with a coffee and paper and wait for the fishing boats to come in.

"Hey, Kevin," she said greeting the owner of the coffee shop.

"Hi, Lissy, long time since we've seen you. How's life up on the tablelands?"

"Pretty good, thanks. How's business?"

"Tourists have been steady and fishing's good. Have you caught up with old Harve yet?"

Shaking her head, Lissy ordered her coffee and gazed out over the ocean. She saw a couple of fishing boats in the southern bay and she tried to concentrate on them rather than the thoughts that were crowding her head. She had blocked them all week and had concentrated on her research. She would love to share this view with Nick. With her chin propped on her hand, she gazed out over the ocean, wondering how it would feel if he were here sharing breakfast with her.

Pushing that thought from her mind, she realised she needed to sort out the situation in her head—and heart—before she went back up the mountain to her life in Armidale. She was so sorry that Tom had got caught up in the middle of her affairs with Nick, but it couldn't be helped. He clearly knew something was going on. She sighed as she tried to analyse her feelings for Nick.

For the life of her, she could not read him. One minute, she was sure that he cared for her and showed how kind and thoughtful he could be. The next moment, he was cold as ice and treated her with contempt. She compared the happy-go-lucky guy of the islands with the cold and unreachable professor at the university. Unless he was in her bed, everything was different.

The wind blew softly from the ocean and Lissy pushed a strand of wayward curls back and sipped her coffee. Since last weekend, she had been trying to fight her strong attraction to him. She would be sensible and apply logic to the situation. A relationship with him would never succeed, even if he did want her.

The attraction was purely physical. As soon as he left her bed, he lost interest in her. It had happened twice, no matter what he said. Each time they slept together, he'd walked out and left her.

So, time to move on and ignore the

attraction ... or just take what he offers and enjoy the sex.

She paid for her coffee and headed back to the beach. Harvey's boat was coming in through the break. When he spotted Lissy waiting on the sand he sent one of his crew up to get the boat trailer and unload the fish boxes. Arms outstretched and a huge grin on his weathered face, Harvey held her tightly for a fishy-smelling hug. His hands held her face and looked closely at her, and he gently flicked his finger on her cheek.

"What are these black circles under your eyes, girl?"

"Big drive down after work last night," she said, grinning back at him.

"Hmm." He stared at her with a frown. "After we've finished here, give me time to get the boat cleaned down, and come back for a coffee. This afternoon we'll have time for a good chat."

As she turned to walk back home, a black motorcycle roared up the hill from the beach and her heart jumped in anticipation, even as she shook her head at her foolish hope. She sauntered back along the sand track to Gramps's cottage, and even though the water would be chilly, she decided to have a swim while she waited for Harvey to get his boat home. Putting on her bikini, she found a clean beach towel and headed back through the dunes to the beach and ran into the waves. The cold water was exhilarating, and she floated on her back, letting the waves wash over her, clearing her mind and gazing at the cloudless sky. Goose bumps eventually sent her from the water and she headed up the beach towards the dunes, away from the north-easterly breeze that was starting to tip the waves with white caps out in the bay.

Flopping onto the towel, Lissy lay on her stomach, with her head on the soft white sand. Her eyes slowly closed. She dozed, drifting in and out of a light sleep, lulled by the sound of the surf and the happy shrieks of children splashing in the waves. The gulls swooped and squawked above the dunes, and the sun warmed her bare skin. Contentment stole over her like a soft blanket as her mind cleared for the first time in days.

Footsteps squeaking in the sand woke her a short time later, and she lay there, eyes closed, enjoying the kiss of the sun on her shoulders. The steps paused, and she slowly opened her eyes to see a pair of tanned, male legs in front of her.

With a groan, she rolled over and sat up, knowing without looking up just who those legs belonged to and understanding that those few minutes of peace had come to an end. Nick walked closer and sat down on the edge of her towel. She reached for her T-shirt and pulled it over her head to cover her bikini.

Hunching her knees up against her chest, she

snapped at him.

"What are you doing here?"

"I asked Mrs. Mac where you were when I couldn't get hold of you this morning." He put his hand on her arm as she attempted to push herself to her feet.

Lissy stood looking down at him and watching warily as he played with handfuls of sand, funnelling it through his fingers as though he didn't have a care in the world. He repeated the action three times without either of them speaking a word until she couldn't stand it any longer. She kneeled down next to him on the towel, her eyes level with his as he played with the sand. She put her hands on his shoulders and felt the instant jolt of heat through her fingertips as she gripped him tightly.

"Nick," she said, enunciating each word clearly as though she was speaking to a child. "You didn't come here to build sandcastles. What are you doing here?"

His hand stilled, and he lifted his eyes to meet hers.

"The simple truth? I had to come. I couldn't stay away from you."

He reached for her and tried to pull her into his arms. Her body trembled as a sudden strength surged through her. She pushed him, and he fell back on her towel as she stood and ran through the dunes, leaving him lying on the sand. The passion she'd experienced with him was already unforgettable and had touched her in ways she had never felt before. If she allowed him to touch her again, she didn't think she would have the strength to face his next rejection.

Much easier to stop him now. She was panting by the time she reached the cottage and she slammed the door shut behind her. Standing at the sink, gripping the edge of the bench, she looked out the window at the big black motorcycle parked in the driveway. Her heartbeat slowly returned to normal as she caught her breath. She reached for the kettle and stood wearily waiting for him to follow her, as she knew he would.

***

Nick waited on the beach for a couple of minutes before he followed her. It was important that he say the right thing to her and not come across as an adolescent with raging hormones. The look on her face had unsettled him; he didn't want to hurt her again.

Because he knew he had.

He walked up the track through the dunes and pushed open the squeaky screen door and entered the old fishing cottage. Waiting beside the door and watching her warily as she stood at an old stone sink, he waited for her to invite him in. He looked at her white knuckles and felt a pang of regret for the distress he always seemed to cause her.

Lissy looked at him for what seemed an eternity before silently pointing to a chair at the old wooden table. As she made a pot of tea, he noticed the tense set of her shoulders and nodded his thanks when she put a tea-stained mug in front of him.

After pouring her tea, she wrapped her hands around her mug before moving across to the other side of the room and sitting on a chair under the window. Her face was flushed and her eyes wide as she sat, with her long, bare legs tucked underneath her; he could see the control she was exerting over her emotions.

She sipped her tea and looked at him over the rim of the mug. "I don't trust you, but I'm going to be honest. I can't think straight when you touch me. You leave me so confused. One minute you want to sleep with me, the next minute you're not talking to me. I won't play these mind games any more. We either have a sexual relationship with mutual honesty or you leave me alone." Her voice was hard. "Stop turning hot and cold and confusing the hell out of me." Placing her mug carefully on the kitchen bench, she stood and put her hands on her hips. "Now tell me, why are you here?"

***

"I was worried about you." Nick stared at her. "I wanted to check you were okay." The guilt was like a brick in his chest and it was overtaking him; the more she seemed to shrink into herself, the worse he felt.

I have to get this sorted out, he thought. *If we just go out for a while, have some great sex and then move on, all this emotional crap will go away.*

"Hah! You didn't come near me all week and then you drive a hundred and fifty kilometres because you're worried about me. Give me a break," she said.

"I deliberately left you alone all week, and then I went to see you. I couldn't find you and Mrs. Mac told me you were down here."

He chuckled ruefully. "But I got poked in the chest by that big umbrella of hers several times while she sternly told me how much I had upset you."

She put her tea on the windowsill and looked outside for a long moment. The sun was dropping behind the trees and the late afternoon sunlight darkened the room, making it difficult to see his expression.

"Why...why? I came to you last Saturday and you threw my feelings back in my face."

"I was ashamed of my behaviour all week. I was scared you would take it as a commitment if I responded to you."

"Did I ask you for commitment?" she asked, her voice frosty. "Me. This is me. Remember, I don't do *commitment*, Nick. You know how I feel about that. I don't believe in the sort of physical attraction we seem to have for each other ending up in any long-lasting relationship."

"I know," he replied. "But I didn't trust you. I thought I could avoid hurting you, but I think I did the opposite." He watched as she wrapped her arms around her chest and appeared to go into self-preservation mode.

"Not at all. I barely gave you a thought. I was busy all week with the research. It's not long till we go the Cook Islands and I have a heap of writing up to do. I will admit I was a little embarrassed about my behaviour at the restaurant, so I kept a bit of a low profile at the university."

Nick knew she was not being honest with him and it amazed him how well he could read her, but he didn't want to push his luck and upset her even more. She turned away from him and looked out the window, her arms still crossed in front of her. There was also no way he was going to let her know that all he wanted to do was come over and hold her. Not sex, just comfort.

"Well," he said. "Now that I know you're okay, I'll head home."

She looked at him, frustration in her eyes.

"You can't...the mountain is closed tonight. Didn't you see the signs at the top? It's closing at night for road work over the weekend from six p.m.

and you won't make it there in time."

He had noticed that on the way down and hadn't given it any thought. All he had been concerned about was making sure she was all right.

"Oh damn ... I forgot."

"You can sleep here and go back up in the morning, if you like."

"That would be great." He stood up slowly and walked over to her, pleased that she'd invited him to stay so readily.

"In the sleepout."

"Of course."

Lissy stared at him as he reached out and tucked a stray curl behind her ear.

He held her gaze and electricity sparked between them.

"Pretty potent combination we make. Let's hope it carries over to our work."

"We can only hope," she said softly.

Nick's eyes dropped to her soft pink lips and he groaned.

It was hard to say who made the first move; he reached for her at the same time she stepped into his arms. He lowered his head as her lips rose to meet his. Her mouth opened to welcome him, and she put her hands into his short hair and pulled him closer. The wind blew the shutter on the kitchen window closed with a loud *bang* and Nick was only vaguely aware of the noise. His hand slid under her shirt and she groaned into his mouth as his fingers caressed the warm silken skin of her back. Her legs wound around his hips as he lifted her onto the bench and kept kissing her until he thought he would expire from lack of breath.

God help me, she is like fire in my blood.

He couldn't keep his hands off her, and a smile tugged at his lips as he realised the feeling was reciprocated, no matter how snarky she had sounded on the beach.

"Not here," she gasped.

"Where's your bedroom?" He lifted her from the bench and followed the direction she pointed in. Kicking open the door with his foot, he carried her into her bedroom and placed her on the bed. "Tell me to stop if this isn't what you want too. And I'll leave."

Lissy's lips met his and he knew what her answer was.

A long time later, she pulled the blanket up over them as the chilly late afternoon breeze blew in through the open window. She turned her back to him as he cradled her to him.

"Lissy—" he whispered, as he nuzzled his lips on her warm skin.

"No words," she replied sleepily. "That's what causes all the trouble between us. Just sleep for a while and then we'll go out and eat." As she drifted off to sleep with a little happy sigh, he stayed beside her and held her soft, warm body close. He had some serious thinking to do.

***

The fragile peace between them didn't last long, and Lissy wasn't surprised. She woke first and had a quick shower before calling Harvey to explain she had an unexpected visitor and she would catch up with him in the morning.

As they ate dinner at the Chinese restaurant in the small coastal town near Blackrock Beach, they skirted around the topic of their relationship and avoided contact of any kind. It was awkward, the way they carefully avoided even brushing fingers as they shared the menu.

Lissy couldn't stand it. The longer they sat there, the more she could see Nick withdraw into himself and her chest tightened, and her appetite fled. The waitress brought their coffee; she looked across at him.

"Well, Nick, this is fun."

He looked up at her.

"It's going to happen again, isn't it?" She tried for a matter-of-fact tone in her voice. "A quick roll in the hay, scratch your itch for the week and off you go again. You have your aloof face back on again."

He put his head in his hands. "What we have frightens me. I don't mean to be aloof."

"Nick, what we have is sex. S...E...X..." Her face heated as the couple sitting at the table next to them paid more attention to her words than to their meal. She lowered her voice. "What upsets me most is the fact that you promise me each time that it won't happen again. You're so predictable and I'm over it."

There was little conversation during the time it took to finish their meals, and as she climbed on the back of the bike and put the spare helmet on, she reluctantly held on to his waist as they took the short trip back to the cottage. Once back, they walked from the driveway to the cottage.

"There's a bed made up on the pull-out couch in the sleep-out. I'm going for a walk."

She turned and walked down the track to the dunes. The full moon hung fat and golden above the horizon, reflecting silver moonlight off the big swells out towards the horizon.

She sat and watched it rise high in the sky, her knees pulled up under her chin. It was almost midnight before she made her way back to the cottage, but she was not surprised to see Nick sitting in the chair on the front porch. Desire had fled as she sat watching the water. The hurt went too deep and she wasn't prepared to trust him. She slowly walked up the steps and stood by him. He reached up and pulled her hair from its ponytail, so that her curls fanned down her back. He buried his head in her curls and put his arms around her.

"I'm sorry I can't promise you anything. I hate hurting you." His voice shook. "I can't stay away from you. You're all I think about. I can't sleep, and my research has come to a standstill."

This was a very different Nick from the confident, sometimes arrogant professor she had worked with for the past few weeks. She leaned her forehead against his.

"I don't want you to promise me anything, Nick. I don't believe in it. I hope when I settle down with someone, it will be based on mutual liking and respect. I don't trust this fire between us. It'll burn itself out."

"Exactly. That's what happened with both Olivia and Rebecca."

He lifted his hand and twirled a curl around his finger, holding her face close to his. "Your hair is magnificent. I love touching it." He put his arms around her and tried to pull her close, but Lissy pushed him away gently, determined not to let him hurt her a second time in one day.

"You're on the pull-out. I'm going to bed. Good night, Nick."

He looked at her, reached over, and ran his finger down her face.

"Good night, Lissy. Sleep well."

She tossed and turned all night.

##

Nick looked at her quizzically the next morning as he straddled his motorcycle ready to make the trip up the mountain. "You're different down here, Lissy. You're in your element...you're like you were in the Whitsundays."

She smiled. "I have the best of both worlds. A great career and it's close enough that I can come home regularly." Nick was staring at her with a strange look on his face.

"You really are happy here, aren't you?"

"Yes, if it makes sense. It's my place. I love being near the water. It gives me peace. I always bolted back here, when I was unhappy at the university. Even though it was an eight-hour train trip, Gramps and the ocean were always waiting for me. It was one of the only certainties in my life."

He reached out and cupped his hand on her cheek. The simple touch set her legs trembling and left her with a need for something she knew he couldn't give to her. The tenderness of his touch and the caring look on his face almost undid her. She turned away from him, so he wouldn't see the longing, which she knew was plainly written across her face.

"Be careful," she said, her voice shaking. "That mountain road is treacherous."

Oh my God. I sound like a wife.

As he roared down the driveway, she gave him a short wave and turned back to the empty cottage. Stripping his bed, she stood for a long time with his pillow against her face, breathing in his distinctive aftershave that lingered on the pillow.

***

An hour later, Lissy walked along the beach to Harvey's shack. The wind had come up and her curls blew into disarray around her face. The temperature dropped as the morning sun disappeared behind the clouds and she rubbed her arms to keep warm. She felt cold both inside and out. She knew Harvey would be in from fishing since the southerly wind had come through, so she was not surprised to see his car and boat parked in the yard at the back of his shack. She helped him unload the fishing gear from his boat and wash it down. After the fish was packed in ice ready for the markets, they sat down for a chat over a pot of tea.

"Okay, young lady, now tell me what you've been up to, and tell me about your biker friend."

Harvey frowned at her across the chipped red laminate table, his bushy eyebrows almost joining. Lissy briefly told him of the events of the past few weeks since she had last seen him at Gramps's service. She sighed, her hands wrapped around the mug.

"There's a bit of an attraction there," she said. "But we're both fighting it for various reasons."

He lifted her chin, with his wrinkled hand and looked into her eyes. "Is he right for you, Lissy?"

"I honestly don't know," she said. "You know how I used to say to Gramps that when the time came I'd choose someone based on sense and security?" She looked at him over the rim of her cup. "I don't know if I think that any more. Even a short relationship would be better than nothing." She spoke more to herself than the old fisherman who was looking at her with concern on his face.

"You know what to do then," he said. "I'll only say one thing to you." He gripped her hands tightly. "It's the same advice that your Gramps always gave you. Follow your heart."

##

Lissy had one more thing to do before she packed up and returned to Armidale. She picked up the phone and dialled her friend from school, the local hairdresser.

"Hi, Kerry. It's Lissy."

"Hey, Lis. Are you home? We haven't seen you for ages."

"Yes, just home for the weekend, but I'm heading up the mountain this afternoon. I have a big favour to ask. Can you fit me in for a haircut this afternoon, before I go back to Armidale?"

***

Lissy drove into the garden of the cottage and quietly unpacked the car. She was relieved to see that Nick's lights were off and the bike wasn't in the carport. She shivered as the cold wind brushed her bare neck. She felt liberated, but strange, without the weight of her curls.

"Not the best hairstyle for Armidale in the winter." Kerry had tried to persuade her to change her mind, but when Lissy had convinced her that it was what she really wanted, she had done a great job. Kerry stood back with the mirror and admired her work. She had cut it short all over.

"Lissy, it makes those green eyes of yours look huge and all the sun gold bits are gone." Lissy looked down at the curls on the floor surrounding her feet and then up to the mirror.

"I love it, Kerry!"

I am a new woman with a firmed resolve.

She gave her friend a hug and promised to catch up for coffee the next time she was home. She didn't leave the coast until mid-afternoon and it was late when she unlocked the cottage, turned the lights on and lit the fire. She hurried over to Mrs. Mac's to pick up Luney and Sylvester.

Mrs. Mac opened the door. "Great timing. I've just cooked some soup for you to take home." She put her hand up over her mouth as Lissy walked in and she saw the short red curls, barely covering her neck.

"Oh, my goodness, young lady, what have you done? Your beautiful hair..."

"A very sudden and knee-jerk decision." She reached her hands up and fluffed the short curls. "Long story—" and she gave her landlady a huge grin, "—but I love it. It feels wonderful."

##

Lissy was eating her soup and laughing at Luney's attempts to get her attention when the telephone rang. Picking it up, she automatically went to hold her hair back behind her ears and laughed when it was not there.

"Melissa McIntyre," she said. There was a slight pause before she heard Tom's voice.

"Hello, Melissa. It's Tom."

She frowned, surprised to hear from him again and her voice was anxious.

"Hello. Is everything all right?" Her first thought was that Nick had not got home safely on that motorcycle.

"Yes, yes. Everything's fine. I have an invitation for you." Tom sounded a little embarrassed.

"Yes?" she replied, her voice guarded.

"Melissa, this is difficult. I know you're angry with Nick and me."

"No," she replied. "I'm not angry."

"Well, Mama is having a barbeque next

weekend because Nick is going to the Islands and she knows you're going too, and she asked me to call and invite you over."

She paused. *Why not.* "That sounds great. I'd love to come."

"Great."

"And," she said. "It'll give us a chance to catch up."

Lissy went to bed feeling more settled and in control of her life than she had for weeks.

The next morning, she dressed in a suit with a turtleneck sweater underneath; she missed the warmth of her hair. The last thing she wanted was to catch a cold before they left for their research trip to the Cook Islands. She carefully made up her eyes, a little more than usual, and found big dangly earrings.

"Not bad, Dr. McIntyre," she said to her reflection in the mirror before she left for work. "Looking confident."

That was not the reaction she got from Nick later that morning. He dropped by her office to see her about some research before morning tea and the loud roar that came from him when he saw her hair brought Jenny running from the reception desk.

"By God, woman." He looked at her in disbelief. "What have you done?" She and Jenny looked at each other and burst out laughing.

"Getting ready for the tropics, Professor."

He glared at her for a minute and then grunted before disappearing into his office.

Chapter Fifteen

Lissy heard laugher and the buzz of happy conversation as she made her way around the back of the Richards's farmhouse on Sunday afternoon. The barbeque had been a hot topic of conversation in the history faculty; many of the staff had been invited and apparently the Richards were renowned for their hospitality. Since it was a casual affair, she had dressed in jeans and an olive-green cashmere sweater that brought out the deep green of her eyes. Her new trademark dangling earrings complimented her short curls. She'd decided as the week progressed that Nick had done her a favour, and she felt liberated by the freedom the short haircut had given her.

Tessa moved towards her as she walked up the steps, hands outstretched in welcome. "My dear, it is wonderful to see you again. Look how beautiful you are."

Lissy touched her short curls as Tessa gently kissed both cheeks, Italian style.

"Amazing what a good haircut can do."

"Thank you, Tessa. you're the only person who likes it!"

Tessa reached up and touched her face with an elegant hand. "It shows off your beautiful green eyes."

Lissy laughed, a little embarrassed by Tessa's attention. "My hairdresser was almost weeping as she cut it."

"I think it looks spectacular," said Tessa, "and if you're happy then that is all that matters." She looped her arm through Lissy's. "Come and meet my nieces. They are visiting from Italy."

Lissy's cheeks warmed and she looked across the garden, sensing someone watching her. Nick was sitting at the table under a tall tree next to an attractive blonde woman, and raised his glass in a silent toast to her.

Tessa followed her gaze. "Don't worry about Nick. He's been in a bad mood all week and we're ignoring him."

Lissy shrugged her shoulders. She knew what his problem was.

If only I could ignore him so easily, she thought.

"Isabella and Talia, this is Melissa, Tom's friend from the university. She also works with Nick, and I've already apologised for his bad mood." Tessa introduced the two young women standing together in the doorway. The girls giggled and the older of the two said, "*Tessa da zia*, we have already met Melissa." They both smiled at her.

"At the restaurant, last weekend."

Lissy laughed with them. "As if I could forget! That was a night to remember. I believe I owe you for finding my keys." The girls spoke perfect English, and as they chatted together, Tom walked around the corner, holding the hand of a small dark-haired young woman.

He looked pleased to see Lissy, came over, and kissed her cheek. "It really is good to see you here." Lissy knew he meant it. He was a great guy and she was sorry she had misjudged him at the restaurant. It looked like it had all blown over and there were no hard feelings. He turned to the young woman by his side.

"Melissa, this is Jill. She just moved back to Armidale and works in the finance department at the university." Jill seemed very shy, and Lissy was pleased to see the coy way that she was watching Tom and that he continued to hold her hand as they stood with the group.

Lissy's neck prickled and she knew without looking that Nick was within her vicinity. She turned and saw him walking over. Before he could reach them, Tessa broke from the group and joined him on the lawn. As the conversation continued around her, Lissy could hear his voice and he sounded angry. She saw him shrug his shoulders and relax as Tessa spoke to him quietly, her hand on his arm. He looked over and saw her watching, and he raised his glass to her again. Tessa gave him a gentle push in the direction of the group gathered on the veranda. Walking over, he stood next to her and said politely, but with no warmth in his voice, "What can I get you to drink, Melissa?"

"White wine, please," she said, smiling brightly at him, determined not to let him ruin her afternoon. He had tried his best to upset her life and career plans, but she had decided it was time to take control. Once the trip to the Cook Islands was over and the research paper was completed, she was going to reconsider her options. Other universities focused on Pacific history research and she would be well placed for an associate professorship after their current paper was published. Leaving Nick behind would be hard, but she had to do it if she wanted any chance at happiness in her life and career.

Nick returned with a glass of wine for her and as she took it, their fingers brushed, and she was surprised that the arc of electricity that flared between them didn't crackle through the air. Conversation flowed around her, and she was content to observe the social interactions of her friends and colleagues. When Sophie, Ally, and Lucy arrived with their families, she was welcomed as an old friend. As more guests arrived, the barbeque livened up and a game of cricket began in the back garden. Lissy moved to a hammock chair on the veranda, content to sit back quietly and watch the game as conversations drifted around her. The smell of meat and onions cooking on the barbeque wafted across the lawn and guests began to drift to the buffet table.

The evening passed pleasantly. Even though it was meant to be a function to get the faculty together before the trip to the Islands, Nick studiously ignored Lissy after giving her the glass of wine. He remained on the far side of the lawn umpiring the cricket game and she took a perverse pleasure in ignoring him back. Despite the tension with him, she enjoyed spending time with her friends from work and left early to go home and pack for the trip.

***

Determined not to let Nick's attitude ruin her trip to the Cook Islands, Lissy welcomed him professionally as they shared a taxi to the airport on Monday morning. Fog had delayed the flight from Armidale to Sydney and they arrived in Sydney with only minutes to spare. They had to run to catch the bus to the international terminal to catch the flight to Rarotonga.

"Why did you wear such high heels?"

She ran along behind him as they sprinted for the bus.

"Faster," said Nick. He held his hand out and she grabbed it. Lissy was thankful their luggage had been checked straight through and she only had a small bag to hold. They picked up their boarding passes at the Polynesian Airlines counter as the flight was called. There was no time for a coffee or a snack before they were called through customs for their passport check.

They boarded the jet and were preparing for take-off. Nick was polite but distant and focused his attention on the cabin staff delivering the safety instructions. Lissy settled into the window seat and took great care in moving as far away from him as she could, which was difficult in the confined space of the shared double seat.

She looked down at the ocean below with her hands clasped tightly on her lap. She'd always had an irrational fear of flying over water. Nick looked across at her and gave her a reassuring smile when he noticed her white knuckles. It was the first smile he had given her since they'd been at Gramps's cottage. She nodded and turned back to the window. Staring at the water, even though it made her feel light-headed, was better than looking at him.

A light meal was served an hour into the flight and after they finished their coffee, Nick was soon immersed in his laptop. Lissy examined him surreptitiously under lowered lids.

His hair had darkened since he had been away from the Pacific and he had lost his tan. The man sitting beside her bore little resemblance to the swaggering sailor she had first met on the yacht two months ago. He looked the part of an academic now and she sensed that it didn't sit comfortably with him. She recalled one of their first true conversations where his love of outdoor adventure and the ocean had been so obvious, and she knew that most of his time at the university was spent in sedentary activities.

No wonder he has been testy and hard to read, she thought. *Being stuck in an office indoors must be hard for him.* She glanced up and realised that Nick was returning the intense scrutiny she had been giving him.

"Everything okay?" he asked.

"Fine," she said. He nodded and looked down at his work.

Lissy put her head back against the soft padding of the seat and closed her eyes.

No matter how terse or rude he was to her, she could not get over the deep attraction she felt for him. She was going to have to move away when they finished their report. She started to daydream about what life would be like if she could trust her feelings for him and he returned that trust.

She slipped into sleep, lulled by the monotonous hum of the engines. As she slept, her lips turned up into a little smile. She fell into a deeper sleep, her head rolling to the side, landing gently on Nick's shoulder.

***

Nick looked down at the short red gold curls tickling his chin. He had been so angry when he saw Lissy's haircut. Not at her, but at himself, because he knew he was the sole reason she'd cut it off. Because he had been foolish enough to say how much he loved running his fingers through her curls...and showing her.

He'd been fighting his feelings for her for weeks. He looked down at her breathing gently and sighed softly before leaning back and closing his eyes. The turmoil of his emotions over the past few months since he'd seen Lissy sitting on the side of the yacht and he had sung that silly ditty to cheer her up, had thrown him. He couldn't remember feeling this emotional in either of his previous serious relationships. Although, he thought with a grimace, he and Lissy were not in a relationship, as she kept reminding him.

And if she had her way they never would be...

Well, how do you feel about that? he thought.

Not good.

She gave a soft little moan and snuggled deeper into his shirt.

Nick's protective instinct kicked in and he

put his arm behind her head and settled her more comfortably into him. She didn't stir. He noticed the dark smudges under her eyes and realised she was losing as much sleep over the situation as he was. He was determined to sort it out this week. Although they would be busy with the final research and writing it up at night, they would still have time to do some serious talking.

I will not touch her all week, he vowed to himself. *We need to step back and get this physical attraction figured out.*

He was ashamed she thought that was all he was in it for.

Chapter Sixteen

Lissy slept until they began their descent into Rarotonga. She stirred, and Nick managed to remove his arm before she woke up.

She looked up at him, her eyes heavy with sleep and her cheeks rosy. "Sorry, I hope I didn't dribble on your shirt."

It had been a long trip and the sun was setting over the ocean as the shuttle pulled up in front of the resort at Avaiki Beach on the western side of Aitutaki. They had travelled by launch from the main island and Lissy felt contentment settle over her as they crossed the water. The majority of their research was on this small island and they had meetings organised in some of the small villages in the centre of the island.

An unspoken truce had sprung up between them, and Nick was polite and responsive to her conversation as the launch ferried them to their final destination.

They were shown to their rooms in the resort by a valet, who advised that their luggage was already there.

"I'll meet you in the bar about seven. Does that work for you?"

She nodded, and the valet showed her to her room. Lissy clapped her hands in delight when she entered her suite. They told her at reception that she had been upgraded because of a double booking. Walking across to the open doors, the front of her room overlooked the lagoon, and she watched in rapture as the sun, a huge golden orb, dropped below the horizon. Stepping out onto her balcony, she was delighted to see her own private lap pool, surrounded by a low fence with a narrow path leading to a private beach.

The balcony and pool were screened by a profusion of tropical colour. Frangipani trees and a myriad of flowering plants that she had never seen before cascaded in a riot of colour down the lattice screen that gave her privacy from the next room. The sweet smell of the blossoms wafted into her room on the light evening breeze.

Stepping back into her room, her eyes widened as she entered the bathroom and saw a huge spa bath set in the floor, with dozens of little candles set into the edge. Two fluffy white robes hung on hooks on the side of the huge clear screen that led into the biggest shower that she had ever seen.

What a waste, she thought with regret. *This is the honeymoon suite!*

Quickly blocking those thoughts, she moved over to her luggage and began to unpack.

I'm not going there. No matter how beautiful it is. We're here to work.

She pulled her laptop from its case and set it up on the desk in the lounge area of the room and checked that the wireless Internet connection was working. Satisfied that she could access her files on the university server if needed, she unpacked her suitcase and had a shower before meeting Nick for dinner.

A pink conch shell on the marble bench in the bathroom overflowed with a variety of bath gels and shampoos. Choosing a black orchid scent, Lissy luxuriated under the steaming shower. Dressing in a pair of loose white pants and pale green top, she put on a minimum of makeup and headed for the bar with a couple of minutes to spare. Steeling herself to meet Nick, she repeated to herself, *we're here to work.*

***

Nick was sitting at the bar waiting for her. He'd already been approached by two attractive women who thought he was alone. Lissy paused at the door and his heart rate kicked up a notch as she walked over to him. The simple colours she wore and the short curls framing her face reminded him of her gentle beauty. She sat on the stool next to him and he looked over at her, his eyes lingering on her face.

"You look very relaxed already," he said.

"Oh, you should see my room. It's fit for a queen! I have a marble spa bath, almost as big as the pool at the indoor sports centre at the university."

He laughed. "That is big, but I'm sure you're exaggerating."

She laughed back at him, and he was pleased to see that they were both playing it the same way.

Friendly, platonic conversation, no touching.

"Well, maybe not quite as big, but you could fit a small family in there."

"Drink?" he asked.

"Yes please, I'm going to have a tropical cocktail, but don't worry, that'll be it for the night. I know we start work in the morning. I'll be up bright and early, ready to go. I'm so looking forward to going into the villages and doing these oral histories."

Nick was touched by her enthusiasm. He had spent so much time in the Islands, it was refreshing to see her excitement about getting in the field and working.

"I was reading some of the tourist literature

in my room." Her eyes sparkled up at him as she sipped her cocktail. "Did you know that Aitutakians believe they descended from Ru, the famous seafaring warrior who sailed from Avaiki? Legend has it he arrived at full moon and he was captivated by its reflection in the vast tranquil lagoon and named his landing point *O'otu*–full moon. That's how the beach here got its name."

"We'll have to talk about that one tomorrow," he replied. He was having trouble taking his eyes from her face. "You really love the ocean, don't you? You seem much happier when you are near the water."

"It was my happy childhood with Gramps and running free at Blackrock Beach. My happiest memories are all to do with the ocean." She sipped her drink and he sensed her withdrawal from him. She put her drink down and turned to him, speaking in a brisk, business-like manner.

"Okay, now tell me the plan for tomorrow."

They discussed the sequence of interviews over dinner and Nick was disappointed when Lissy refused his offer of a walk along the beach after dinner.

"Thanks, but I have some work I want to do and some emails to send." He watched as she stood and left the restaurant. Nick finished his drink, signed the bill for dinner and headed out to the beach for a walk.

##

The next morning, they were picked up bright and early by a driver in a brightly-coloured four-wheel drive vehicle to head for Tomara, the first village they were visiting. Nick slid a small tray of bottled water into the back of the vehicle with their laptops.

"Where's the recording equipment?" asked Lissy, surprised to see him traveling so lightly.

"Don't need it," he said. "My laptop has a special external microphone that will record across a room and pick up individual voices in even the noisiest of rooms."

Lissy turned her attention to the road as the driver pulled on to the dirt road. They arrived in the village after a short drive and she smiled as she saw the young children running towards them. The Cook Islanders were an extremely happy people and the driver informed them that the village had been looking forward to the professor's visit.

"*Kia orana*, professor." The chief held both hands out in welcome to Nick.

Nick reached out and grasped the chief's hands, but the old man pulled him in and enveloped him in a back-slapping embrace.

"Come, come." The chief led them across to a rectangular ceremonial building, decorated with ornate carvings. The doorway was low and even Lissy had to lower her head to walk through the intricately carved doorway. They were greeted by the excited voices of a group of women, sitting in a circle in the centre of the room. Waves of brightly coloured fabric covered their legs and spread across the floor of the room as they stitched with fine needles. Lissy walked to the edge of the circle and pointed to the fabric and asked what the women were making.

"*Tivaeva*." A young woman gestured for her to sit with them. She looked across at Nick and the chief nodded his head vigorously.

"You bring your wife too, professor?" He slapped Nick on the back good-naturedly. "Welcome, Mrs. Professor." She opened her mouth to correct him, but Nick glanced across and shook his head almost imperceptibly.

She glared back at him, confused by his direction as the young woman pulled her down to join the circle on the wooden floor. Lissy looked closely and realised the brightly coloured fabrics were patchwork quilts, overlapping each other. One of the older women must have noticed the surprise on her face.

"This is the meeting hall and the *vainetini*. Our group of women from the village meet here in the mornings to do *Tivaevae*. Our islands are famous for the magnificent bed covers we sew; they are very popular with the tourists." She held up the one she was stitching. "They are given to important guests as gifts. This is for you and your professor husband to take home. It is good for fertility." The other women giggled.

Lissy shook her head and stood, moving across to join Nick as the chief invited them both to drink juice from a carved wooden bowl and eat from a platter of fresh fruit. She watched with interest as some of the women began to sing while they stitched.

When they finished eating, Nick leaned across to the chief. "Are you ready for us to set up our equipment and start recording?"

The chief nodded. Nick booted up his laptop and set it up on the low table in the middle of the building, the webcam pointing towards the chief. The chief called over two more old men and nodded at Nick. The men sat cross-legged on the woven mat next to the chief and Nick pushed Lissy gently behind him. He asked the first question and settled in comfortably as the chief spoke for a few minutes without pause.

He described how the women would leave the meeting room at midday and the men would come in and spend the afternoon working on wood carvings, but one of the other men explained it had lost its spiritual and cultural emphasis and was now mainly for the tourists to purchase.

Each time Lissy tried to ask a question, Nick raised his hand and stopped her before she could say a word. The chief nodded and thumped Nick on the back as he let out a deep booming laugh.

Her temper simmered. She sat there for two hours and didn't say a word and couldn't get anywhere near the laptop. Eventually, the women gathered their fabrics, left, and the chief stood indicating that it was time to eat. He pointed out the ablutions block to Nick and invited them to freshen up for the meal.

As soon as he left the building, Lissy stood up and marched over to Nick, who was packing up his laptop.

He turned, his hands raised in front of himself for protection.

"All right, Mr. Professor, would you like to tell me what that was all about? You knew before you started that I wouldn't be saying or doing anything. Why did you need a research assistant on this trip? What ulterior motive did you have?" Her voice rose with each question. "I can't trust you, can I?" Lissy pushed him in the chest and took a step back as she saw the anger flare in his face.

"While we are talking trust, let's talk about you! You're the one with the trust issues, Melissa."

She knew with the 'Melissa' that he was really angry.

"It wasn't the chief I was expecting," he said. "The adviser warned me that it depended on which of the four chiefs we saw. He said to me that if we had this one, he would not speak to a woman.

That's why I didn't want you to talk and I let him believe you were my wife."

"I didn't do my doctorate to be decoration!" Lissy was trying to stay calm, but her temper was taking over.

"Keep your voice down," he said. "I don't want to blow this before we finish."

"Well, you can stay here and finish," she said pushing to her feet, hands on hips. I'm getting the driver to take me back to the town. I have plenty of work I can do in the historical museum."

"Whatever," he said dismissively. "I don't care what you do. You're too hard to follow."

"Well," Lissy replied. "I don't care what you do either!" She glared at him and picked up her bag and laptop, walking out to the car with as much dignity as she could muster. The driver was sitting under a leafy mango tree, his hat pulled over his eyes. She stood there and cleared her throat to get his attention, but he didn't stir.

"Ahem."

Nick walked to the door of the building and stood and leaned against the carved wood entry, watching her, his expression inscrutable. Lissy stood over the driver and shook his shoulder. "I'm sorry to wake you. I want to go back to the town. Can you drive me please?"

The man scrambled to his feet and opened the car door for her. With a last glare over her shoulder at Nick, she slammed the car door and they headed down the hill back towards the coast. As the vehicle rattled and bounced over the rutted track, her anger threatened to overwhelm her. She had not been so angry for a long time—Nick brought out a temper that she thought she had outgrown many years before. The anger settled like a cold stone in her chest. Nick managed to make her feel absolutely useless. It was not the fact that the chief wouldn't speak to her that upset her; it was the fact that he had known and not mentioned it. He knew she would not have travelled with him if that was the case.

It made her question the entire reason he had wanted her to come to the Islands with him. *Does he have any respect for my work at all?*

She had a quick lunch at the buffet in the dining room, freshened up and grabbed her laptop, heading for the museum. Despite Nick and his games, there was plenty of additional material she could glean from local sources. She could start the research she had planned for later in the week now, and if she finished earlier she would change her flight and leave him here.

She had set up a database with the research that she was finalizing and had many records that needed updating from primary source material at the local museum. A tall islander with a friendly face greeted her as she knocked on the office door at the back of the building.

"Dr. McIntyre, how wonderful to meet you. I have read some of your publications on our Islands and love reading your theories, especially the one about—" He broke off and smiled.

"Oh, I'm being rude, I'm so sorry. My name is James Toki." He reached out and took her hands in his as he introduced himself. "I studied in Sydney and Auckland and came back here to my home. I think you will be pleased with the recent progress we have made on dating the first arrivals and tracking their journeys."

Lissy spent a pleasant afternoon with Jim, as he insisted she call him. It was a refreshing change to be respected for her research and her professional standing. It made her realise Nick considered her from a physical and emotional point of view only. Although, she did concede that perhaps she was being too harsh. He had always shown the utmost respect for her work at the university. She shook her head angrily—she was sick of him messing with her thoughts and emotions.

Glancing down at her watch, she realised she had kept Jim way past the closing time.

"Oh dear," she said. "I've kept you for too long."

"It's been a pleasure," Jim said.

"I have so much more to ask you about the information I collected this afternoon. May I come back tomorrow?"

"How about dinner tonight?" Jim looked down at her. For a brief moment, Lissy worried about Nick's reaction and then cast it aside.

"That would be great."

"Where are you staying? At the resort on the beach?" When she nodded in agreement, Jim reached out and shook her hand. "I will come and join you there if that suits you. About seven?"

"That would be fine. I look forward to it." She couldn't help but be aware of the admiration in his eyes as he bid her good afternoon and closed the museum up. She strolled along the beach back to the resort, satisfied with her afternoon's work.

Lissy went back to her room, stripped down, put on her bikini and did a number of laps in the private pool on her balcony. After drying off with one of the luxurious beach towels, she took a beer out of the fridge in her room and sipped it as she gazed at the magnificent view across the lagoon.

Mmm, I could get used to this.

She picked up her laptop and stretched out on the deckchair next to the pool. She started to read through her notes from the morning, trying to push away the little fingers of guilt that were trailing across her mind. She felt as though she should explain to Nick what she was doing and where she was.

Damn him. Even though he had been the

cause of her bad mood, and her leaving the village, she'd had a productive afternoon despite his arrogant attitude. She probably could have found out the information from the museum by email from the university in Armidale.

But I wouldn't be lying here in the warm sun, looking forward to a dinner date with a good-looking guy tonight.

The sun warmed her back as she dozed and thought about Nick and Jim. They were both great-looking guys, so why the attraction to Nick and not to Jim? Tall and dark-skinned, Jim had a killer smile, a keen intelligence, and the same research interests as she did, but she had not felt one jolt of physical attraction to him. On the other hand, she thought angrily, one thought of Nick drifted into her mind and her body turned into a quivering mess.

What is it about the man that causes me so much grief?

Lissy lay in the sun, and the combination of the warmth and the beer lulled her into a light doze.

Chapter Seventeen

After a productive morning interviewing the chief and his sons, Nick finally returned to the hotel. Dropping off his laptop and rucksack in his room, he made his way to Lissy's room. He grimaced as he remembered her anger and the baleful glare she had sent him as the four-wheel drive vehicle had bounced out of the village. Tapping lightly on her door, he waited patiently so he could deliver his apology. He knocked a little louder, but there was still no answer. He listened; all was quiet. Shrugging, he made his way to his room to write up his notes. She must have gone exploring, so he would apologise over dinner.

A couple of hours later, Nick logged off, stretching and rolling his stiff shoulders. He couldn't wait to tell Lissy of the progress he had made today. The information he had written up would speed up the finalization of their research and they would be finished sooner than he had hoped. He would be free to move on and leave Armidale and head back out to the Islands once the research report was written and published.

He frowned to himself as the reality of leaving Armidale and returning to the Islands on a permanent basis filled him with dismay.

That's what I want, isn't it? Yep, get away from all this emotional stuff.

Now it was time to go to the bar and hope Lissy would speak to him, so he could make up for the misunderstanding today.

She was sitting on a stool at the bar, her tinkling laugh drifting across to Nick as he walked in past the pool. A silk dress clung softly to her curves, her lightly tanned shoulders contrasting with the gold hues of her dress. A tall man leaned in close to Lissy, in an intense conversation as she sipped on a cocktail with a little umbrella poking from the side.

"To fortuitous meetings." The words drifted across to Nick standing at the door. Nick walked across the tiled floor to the bar, his eyes on Lissy.

***

Lissy sensed Nick's mood as he approached the bar. She sighed and closed her eyes, waiting for the harsh words. He was so predictable, she could read him like a book and he was spitting fire. She could see it in his eyes and his shoulders.

He walked over to join them and before Lissy could introduce Nick to Jim, they greeted each other by name. A lot of backslapping and banter ensued.

"Jim and I worked together in Auckland a few years back," Nick said, turning to Lissy.

"If you could call it work," Jim said laughing. "It was more party, party, party, if my memory serves me correctly."

She listened politely as they caught up on mutual acquaintances.

Nick looked across at her at her and asked if it was okay by her if Jim joined them for dinner.

"Well, actually—" she started to say.

Jim took pity on Nick and interrupted. "I'd be delighted to, man. I'm sure Lissy is okay with that." Jim turned and winked at her.

It was an enjoyable evening and much discussion took place on their research project, leaving little time for personal discussion. When they bid Jim farewell, Lissy said goodnight to both men and turned to leave.

Nick took her arm.

"Dr. McIntyre, there are some things we need to discuss about today's interviews."

Lissy's arm burned where Nick held her. Jim said good-bye to them both, oblivious to any tension, and left, promising to catch up with them before they left the island. Nick continued to hold her arm.

"Will we walk and talk, or will you come to

my room?" he asked.

She pulled her arm from his grasp, turned and said sarcastically, "Oh no, not again. You've already exhausted that line. I won't fall for it twice."

He nodded tersely. "We'll walk."

They stepped from the restaurant onto the sand and Lissy reached down and slipped her high sandals off. Nick put his shoes next to hers and their fingers brushed as they reached across to the grass. She pulled back crossly as though her fingers were burned and felt a degree of satisfaction when she saw the frown on his face.

The soft white sand was still warm to their bare feet. They walked past the Polynesian flares that flamed in the soft breeze lighting the path along the beach. The sighing of the waves breaking on the beach filled an uncomfortable silence. The shadows cast by the flames highlighted the gold in Lissy's curls and Nick's stomach clenched with desire. He reached out for her hand and pulled her over to a seat on the edge of the lawn overlooking the moonlit lagoon.

"Sit down...please." He sat beside her and stared out at the water. "I'm sorry about today. I took too much for granted. I'm used to working alone. I didn't think about how much it would upset you. I usually think too much about you and my feelings, but no matter what I do it seems to upset one of us." He reached over and flicked his fingers through her short curls, looking at her trying to read the expression on her face.

"How are we going to get some equilibrium in our relationships, Lis?"

She looked across at him and tentatively reached out and placed her hand on his.

"It's all right. I can understand what happened. I overreacted. It's all about communication."

"Let me communicate with you now," he said, his voice rough. "Let me tell you how I felt when I walked in and saw you laughing it up with Jim. I felt like I had been kicked in the gut." He squeezed her fingers. "I was so jealous. All I could think was, 'Why can't she look at me like that?'"

"It's simple." Her voice was soft, and he had to bend closer to hear what she was saying. She looked back at him, her expression serious. "Physically, we are attracted to each other; however, our minds and emotions are not involved. We have trust issues. We can't be involved because intellectually and sensibly we both know it's not what either of us want out of life."

She looked at him, and her voice shook with emotion. "I don't believe that any relationship between us would last and you don't trust me, anyway, even if I wanted a relationship with you.

So, I'm not going to sleep with you anymore because it isn't doing either of us any good. No matter..." Her eyes filled with tears and she reached up to cup his face as she held his gaze. "No matter how much I want to."

The sadness on her face dispelled all desire and calmness descended over him.

"We're a sad pair, aren't we? Wouldn't it be easier to give in and see where it takes us?"

"No way," she said, moving away from him and crossing her arms in front of her soft breasts. "It would give us a lot more grief in the long run."

She stood. "I'm going to bed now. I'll see you in the morning."

He knew she was slipping away from him and maybe, just maybe, it was too late to win her back.

Lissy ran lightly across the sand to the grass, picked up her sandals and disappeared along the path to her room.

***

Lissy tossed and turned all night and came to a decision. When the research report was finished and the publication underway, she was going to look for an associate professorship at another university. It was time to spread her wings anyway. She would look for something in New Zealand or North Queensland where she could continue her research in Pacific history.

Feeling better now that she had reached a decision, she headed off to the restaurant for breakfast. Half an hour later, sitting at a table that overlooked the lagoon to the west and the garden rooms between the balcony and the sand, she still could not help herself glancing across towards Nick's room, hoping he would join her for breakfast. As she sipped pungent Brazilian coffee and nibbled on a sinfully rich pastry, she tried to focus her mind on the research she had to finish and forget about the man who was causing her so much confusion.

Chapter Eighteen

The week in the Cook Islands had flown by and Nick and Lissy had arrived in Sydney late yesterday afternoon. The call for their connecting flight to Armidale came over the loudspeakers and Nick picked up his bag and turned to Lissy.

"Ready?" He was polite, as she had not spoken to him about anything other than work-related matters since their walk by the lagoon. She had worked on her laptop on the flight from Rarotonga to Sydney, and when the battery power had run out, had pulled out a novel from her bag and remained immersed in that until they landed.

Lissy looked at him. "Oh, I meant to tell you. I'm flying to Coffs Harbour. I'm going home for the weekend."

He felt bereft at the thought of getting on a plane without her by his side after spending the whole week with her. He reached out and put his hand on her shoulder before he headed for the steps down to the tarmac. She flinched.

"Are you okay getting back up the mountain

on Sunday? Do you want me to come and get you?" he asked.

"Thank you, but I've already made arrangements to come back up on Sunday night. Have a safe trip. I'll see you Monday in the office." She turned back to her book and he felt summarily dismissed. He walked slowly to the flight attendant at the counter, boarding pass clenched tightly in his hand. It took all of his willpower not to look back at her. His jaw was clenched, and he had a feeling of impending doom in his chest. Something was wrong. It was not in Lissy's nature to be cold and dismissive.

##

Nick rose from the chair in front of the fire and walked over to the windows overlooking the lawn where he'd played cricket and tumbled with his brothers and sisters when they were kids. Tessa walked in with two cups of coffee and broke his reverie. The smell of freshly baked scones enticed him to join her by the fire.

My heart may be breaking, but I still have my appetite. He shook his head angrily. *Where did that come from?*

"Now, tell me about your trip to those beautiful islands. And then I want to know why you are so sad." He reached for a warm pumpkin scone and savoured the taste of the treat drenched in butter.

"Comfort food for me, Mama?"

"Yes," she said. "I do not like to see any of my children unhappy. You have not been your happy-go-lucky self since you came back to the university. You have become *uomo anziano irritabile*." She reached over and placed her hand on his tanned arm.

"It is Melissa who makes you so sad, isn't it?"

He leaned over, ignoring her question and put his head in his hands, impatiently brushing his shaggy hair back from his eyes.

"Time for another haircut, Mama."

"Don't change the subject," she said. "I am not going to let it go. I want to know what is going on."

It was a relief to finally let it all out. "It's Lissy, Mama, not Melissa and not Dr. McIntyre. She is driving me crazy. We didn't have the best start."

He told her about their meeting in the Whitsundays, and Tessa indicated she was not surprised that they had met before.

"I knew as soon as I saw the fireworks between the two of you that first night Tom brought her to meet us that you already knew each other. The fireworks almost lit up the veranda, but she looked so sad."

"I feel bad about that. I think Tomas was

serious about her," Nick said.

Tessa laughed. "In his life planning maybe, but there was no spark between them. Besides, there is the lovely Jill, and I can see the beginning of a spark there. Tomas is much more reserved than you. You have always shown your emotion, no matter how serious a professor you think you may be."

He looked at her and groaned. "So, the whole family knows?"

"Only your sisters and I have noticed. It has been the subject of some lively discussion between us when we have coffee. There is a bet on when you will get together."

Nick burst out laughing. "Mama, you are incorrigible and you encourage my sisters to be the same. However, the bet won't be won."

Tessa sat on the side of his chair and put one hand on his shoulder.

"Why are you frightened, son?"

Thoughts scattered through his mind as he tried to find the simplest reply that would convince her that he could not have a relationship with Lissy.

"I can't trust my feelings, Mama. I was so let down by Olivia and Rebecca. I can't trust that Lissy won't leave me as well. Besides, even when I've offered my heart to her, she doesn't trust me. She doesn't believe in love, and neither do I."

"Pfffft." Tessa dismissed him, her hands accompanying her words with a very European gesture.

"Listen to me, my son." He looked at her as she took his face between her beautifully manicured hands.

"You were young when Olivia left you, and I never saw you look at her like I see you look at Melissa. You only thought you were hurt by Rebecca. Your pride was hurt both times. Both of those young ladies were astute enough to realise that there was no enduring love to be had with you. But with your Lissy, it is different. The electricity crackles between the pair of you, even when you are on separate sides of the room. Tell me, son, how would you feel if you thought you were never going to see her again?"

He looked at his mother for a long moment without answering and eventually Tessa stood and gathered the cups. As she walked to the kitchen, she said, "Take some time to think about that, Nick."

What his mother was telling him about Lissy was the truth; he knew that in his heart. He walked to the window and gazed out over the green lawn, his heart in turmoil. Lissy hadn't lied to him; she had been true to herself from the beginning. The problems had been caused by his lack of trust, in both himself and in Lissy. He had accused her of manipulation and deceit.

Well done, you idiot.

Sunday night, he thought. I will be waiting

for her when she comes home. *We're going to talk about this once and for all...but with absolute trust and honesty.*

He bid his mother farewell and headed for the university to work on his research report, much happier than he had been for weeks.

Chapter Nineteen

Lissy had not told Nick at the airport that she was coming back to Armidale with her mother and Lars on Sunday night. She hadn't even mentioned to him that they were coming from Denmark to visit her. During the short flight from Sydney to Coffs Harbour, she focused on seeing her mother at the airport. She had received an email two days ago letting her know that they had completed the first leg of their trip safely and would arrive in Sydney a day before Lissy flew back from the Cook Islands.

We'll hire a car and drive up to Blackrock, and then we can give you a lift up to Armidale on Sunday night. Lissy, we can't wait to see you. Love, Mum

She was also excited about seeing her mother. It had been almost two years.

Lissy disembarked at Coffs Harbour airport and walked through the avenues of tropical plants lining the entry to the terminal. She saw her mother waving madly through the observation window.

Crossing through the automatic doors into the terminal, Lissy saw everyone around them smile as her mother squealed with delight and ran across the waiting area to grab her daughter in a huge hug. Lissy couldn't hold back the tears...and she didn't try to. After many hugs and kisses from her mother, she stepped back.

"Look at you, Mum. You look fantastic. Everyone will think you're my sister, not my mother."

Lyn reached over and touched Lissy's short curls. "What's this, where have your beautiful curls gone?"

Lissy grimaced, a fleeting dart of pain overshadowing the reunion with her mother.

"Long story, Mum. I'll tell you over coffee." She looked up at the huge man standing behind Lyn. Lyn turned proudly and pulled him over. "Lis, this is Lars." Lyn looked up at him and Lissy could see the love in her eyes as her mother said simply, "He's the love of my life."

The huge man who towered over her petite mother reminded Lissy of a grizzly bear. He was all brown–brown hair, a thick brown beard, and a brown shirt. Lars reached out and her hands were engulfed in his huge grasp.

"I'm so very pleased to meet you. Your mother has chattered non-stop about you since the day she met me."

Her mother stood and beamed at the pair of them. "Come on," she said, linking her arm with Lissy, "come and get your luggage and then we have a surprise for you."

They retrieved Lissy's bags from the carousel and made their way out to the parking lot.

Instead of heading for the cars parked behind the security fence, Lyn and Lars turned and walked to the fifteen-minute parking bay. Lissy was delighted to see Harvey standing next to his four-wheel drive fishing vehicle. He held his arms open and she ran in for a big hug.

"Harvey offered to drive us up. Lars has found driving on the wrong side of the road rather terrifying."

"She smells a bit fishy, Lis, but the old girl will get us back to Blackrock," said Harvey, laughing. Lars and Lyn climbed into the back and Lissy sat up in the front with Harvey.

She reached back and gave her mother's hand a squeeze. It was so wonderful to see her. She looked over the front seat and was surprised to see Lyn and Lars holding hands like teenagers. She turned back to the front of the car, thoughtful.

He's certainly different from my other stepfathers.

Lyn and Lissy talked into the early hours after stopping at the local Chinese restaurant and having dinner with Harvey on the way home. "Lars is wonderful, Mum." Lissy gave her approval and Lyn visibly relaxed as her face lit up.

"Oh, it's something so special. For the first time in my life, I'm truly in love and I feel loved and cherished. Lars would do anything for me and I adore him. We have some news."

"Mum—" Lissy looked at her mother aghast. "—you're not..."

Lyn giggled like a teenager. "God, no. Way too old for that. Lars has two grown children and I have you. Our family is complete. No, it's even more exciting than that. Harvey and Lars have been talking. Lars has a fishing boat, and he fishes out of Frederickshavn, where we live in the summer. Harvey is looking for a new crewman to help him out, so we're going to spend six months in Denmark and then come over here for the summer each year, and Lars will fish on Harvey's boat."

Lissy's eyes filled with tears and she reached over to hug her mother. "Mum, that is the best news ever." Once the tears started, she couldn't stop them, and she snuggled into her mother's comforting shoulder. Lyn gently patted her short curls.

"I knew something was wrong. Harvey told me you hadn't been happy, and you're too thin. What is it, darling?"

Lissy cried even harder. Her happiness with her mother's news was overlaid by her grief for

Nick and the lost relationship that never was. She told her mother all about Nick and how even if he had wanted her, she wouldn't commit to him.

Her mother pushed her gently away and held her gaze. "Did you ever wonder why you can't trust a man enough to have a serious relationship?" She spoke softly. "You have to trust love and it sounds to me as though you are in love."

"I don't understand how you can be so trusting, Mum. Look at your relationships, your marriages. Nothing—" she rubbed angrily at her tear-streaked cheeks, "—nothing ever lasts." She pulled away from Lyn and walked over to the kitchen window, looking out into the darkness.

Lyn walked back over to her daughter and placed her hands on either side of her face. "Lissy. Look at me...tell me what you see. Really look at me."

The tears clogged Lissy's throat and she stifled another sob.

"I see somebody who is happy and very much in love. I see Lars look at you and realise that he is protecting you and—"

"Exactly. I love him, and he loves me. Do you remember what Gramps used to say? Wait for your destiny. It will find you. Well, I didn't wait. I married Declan because I was pregnant with you. What we had together was fun, and I don't regret one minute of it, because it gave me you. Then Greg came along, and I could see the security he could provide for us. When he left me for his secretary, I wasn't surprised. We really didn't have a close relationship. There was no spark. I'm a slow learner and poor Lincoln came in on the rebound. But, darling girl, please believe me now. When love arrives, and sometimes from the most unexpected direction, you will know it. You can't live your life and make decisions based on my experiences. Heed what Gramps used to tell us. He was a wise man and he and your grandmother knew true love for almost fifty years." She walked over to Lissy and turned her around, reaching up to wipe her eyes.

Lissy reached for a tissue, blew her nose loudly and summoned up a watery smile.

"Now...you are a smart young woman, with your career taking off. You think about what you want out of life. Have you been lonely since Gramps died and a bit of attention from your Nick has got you sucked in?"

Lissy went to bed and slept deeply and dreamlessly. Rising late, she was sitting on the porch with her coffee as Lyn and Lars walked back from the beach, arm in arm. She watched as Lars picked her mother up and kissed her, and they stood together in the sand dunes, watching the ocean. The love between them was obvious and Lissy realised it was the happiest she had ever seen her mother.

It's the best news ever.

They walked through the gate, laughing and greeting Lissy with a good morning kiss.

"My turn to cook up a big Aussie breakfast," said Lissy. "You look hungry, Lars." As she bustled around in the kitchen, Lissy paused and turned to Lyn.

"Mum, I have a big favour to ask."

Lyn looked across at her.

"I'll come back and help you with Gramps's things next weekend. I was hoping that you would give me a lift to Coffs Harbour this afternoon."

Lyn looked at her, a knowing look in her eyes.

"I'm going to hire a car and go back up the mountain to Armidale this afternoon. I've made some big decisions and I have some important things to see to." Lyn looked up at Lars who nodded happily.

"I'll come along and keep your mother company when she drives back from Coffs Harbour after you have gone back up your mountain."

Lissy laughed. "Lars, if only you knew I am climbing more than one mountain!"

Lyn reached over and pulled her into a hug. "I can't wait to meet him."

"We'll see, Mum. We'll just have to wait

and see."

***

It was early afternoon by the time they finished breakfast, cleaned up and drove up the winding Pacific Highway to Coffs Harbour. Traffic was heavy as they pulled into the car rental place on the north side of town; the winter school holidays had begun, and a light rain was falling.

"You be careful driving up that mountain, Lis. The road will be slippery."

"It's okay, Mum. I'm used to it." She smiled at Lars. "You be careful driving Lars up tomorrow. He's used to the flatlands of Denmark. It may be a bit scary for him." She hugged them both and waved them off. She went in to collect the keys for the rental car that she had arranged by telephone earlier in the day. Lissy stowed her luggage in the small hatchback and left for Armidale, determined to sort it out with Nick before the day was done. She had accepted she was in love with him and even if he didn't want to hear it, she was going to be honest. The problem for the past few months had been her lack of honesty and trust, and that had gotten them nowhere.

By the time she turned the little car off the coastal highway, it was late afternoon and a storm was brewing in the mountains. She hated driving in that twilight between dusk and dark, and switched her headlights onto high beam. The rain started to pour as she drove slowly through the little town of Bellingen at the base of the mountain. She pulled over to get a coffee. The traffic coming towards her was heavy as school holiday traffic travelled from the Western Plains and the New England tablelands for a warm winter holiday on the coast.

She started up the mountain and the rain eased a little. Relaxing into the drive and reached over to turn the music on. When she took her eyes from the road, a large car crossed to her side of the road, the bright headlights blinding her for a moment. Lissy yanked the steering wheel to the left and sighed with relief as the car passed her safely. She relaxed too soon, and the wheels of her small car slid in the soft mud at the side of the road. Suddenly a steep precipice loomed in front of her. Lissy screamed as the car lurched over the gaping drop and slammed head-on into a large tree on the edge of the cliff.

***

Drip. Drip. Drip.

Lissy opened her eyes, confused, not knowing where she was and why there was water dripping on her face. Her limbs trembled with shock; it was pitch dark. She tried to sit up, but the pressure of the seat belt across her chest held her back. She reached for the interior light and switched it on, but all that did was light the interior of the car.

She couldn't see outside or where she was. Her head felt cold; when she touched it, her hand came away covered in blood. Her heartrate picked up and she panicked.

Take a deep breath, calm down.

Lissy reached up and felt for the damp patch in her hair. Feeling a little bit ill, she gingerly explored the wound and realised it was only a small cut. She stretched and tested her arms and legs, and understood it was the bump on her head that had knocked her out. Her head must have hit the side of the small car when it lurched over the mountainside. The seat-belt latch had cut her scalp when she slammed into the side of the car. Reaching for her phone to call for help, she pressed the on button before she remembered there was no service on the mountain. About to throw it aside, she decided to send a text since sometimes they would get through as the service came in and out.

But to whom?

She didn't know Nick's number. She had never needed to call him, working in the same building and living next door to him. She scrolled through the numbers on her phone and Tom's number flashed up. She sent a brief text message.

I'm OK but have had an accident. Gone over the mountain about three kms up. Help please.

Desperately, she prayed the message would go through. She was about to put the phone down when she remembered the flashlight app. Turning off the interior light of the car, she turned on the flashlight and shone it through the window. All she could see was the leaves and tree trunks of the rainforest.

Please God, let me be wedged securely. Reaching for the tissues in her bag, she formed a cotton wad and pressed it against the wound on her head. After a few minutes of pressure, it came away with only a small amount of blood. She leaned back and tried to rest. Her head was thumping, and she was a little worried about a concussion. She couldn't see any lights or hear any other vehicles, so she figured she must be a fair way over the side down in the thick rainforest.

Drip. Drip. Drip.

The smell of fuel wafted through the car as the dripping got louder. Undoing her seat belt and putting her phone in her pocket, Lissy slid over to the door. She opened it carefully, shone her torch out and saw that the front wheels of the car were wedged in a tree. The rear of the car was hanging over a huge black drop. Her choices were to stay in the car with the dripping gasoline or try to get out and clamber down the tree without falling down that huge drop.

She turned the flashlight off to save her battery and put her wallet in the deep front pocket of her jeans. The rest of her luggage didn't matter.

She carefully climbed through the open door, gripping the roof of the car as she slid out and shone the flashlight into the tree. A huge branch was butted up against the side of the car and she was able to climb out of the door and put her arms around the branch as she stepped to a horizontal branch a meter down.

I have to get down in case the car catches on fire.

Looking into the dark and feeling the misty rain dripping onto her hair and neck, she gripped the tree trunk and slid down. It seemed she was only a few metres up and it wasn't too difficult making her way down, although her hands and arms were soon scratched by the sharp prickles on the leaves. When her feet landed on the ground at the bottom of the tree, her legs slipped out from under her in the mud and she slid to the bottom of the slope, losing her phone.

I have to stay awake.

She touched the wound and her fingers stayed dry. It had stopped bleeding, although her head was aching. She felt cold mud on her legs and shivered as she thought of the leeches and the snakes that abounded in the rainforest. Hysteria bubbled up in her throat and she fought to swallow it down and remain calm. She had no idea where she was, which way was east or west, or which was the best way to get out of the forest and back up to the road. Listening carefully over the whoosh of the wind in the trees, she heard the river. If she made her way down to the river it would eventually bring her back to the road.

Blocking the thought of snakes and leeches, Lissy headed off in total darkness, walking towards the sound of the running water. She walked for a long time in the dark, slipping and sliding and falling many times until she finally reached the side of the Bellinger River. The water was flowing across the stony riverbed and she reached in with scooped hands and had a big drink of icy cold water. Her legs were too tired to go any farther and the thumping in her head had become unbearable. She was wet and muddy, and the shivering had taken over her arms and legs; Lissy couldn't stop her teeth from chattering. She sat down, leaned against a tree, and tried to fight the sleepiness that was stealing over her.

I must stay awake.

She drifted in and out of sleep. Her heart beat in time with the dripping of the rain that pierced the thick foliage of the trees above the muddy slope next to the river. Fingers of cold touched her legs and she screamed as the first leech pierced the warm flesh of her thigh. Lissy jumped up, her head spinning, and tried to get her bearings. She walked some more and saw headlights in the far distance on the road that snaked along the bottom of the mountain alongside the river.

Chapter Twenty

Nick heard the running footsteps on his veranda seconds before there was a frantic knocking at the door. He opened the door to see Tom about to knock again and Tessa running up the steps behind him. His first thought was that Lissy was in trouble. He had been listening for her arrival all night and was starting to worry.

"Nick, it's Lissy," said Tom.

Nick's mouth was dry, and his heart thudded rapidly as he looked from his brother to Tessa. He knew it was bad.

"There's been an accident." Tessa reached out and took Nick's hands between hers. "How bad is it?" Nick's voice shook, and he cleared his throat. "Tell me ... where is she?"

He grabbed his keys and helmet and strode to the door.

"No. I'll drive. You can't take the bike." Tom grabbed his arm and pulled him away from the door. Tessa walked over and put her arms around him.

"Sit down for a minute and calm down and

we'll tell you what happened."

"Mate..." Tom put his hands on Nick's shoulders. "I got a text from Lissy. She's gone over the mountain. She must be okay, Nick. She was able to send me a text."

"How long ago?"

"Four o'clock," said Tom.

"Why the hell didn't you come and get me sooner?" Nick yelled. He stood and pulled away from Tessa.

"My phone was in my briefcase and the text was four hours old before I received it. Calm down. I've called the Bellingen police and they're out looking for her already. It'll take us a good hour and a half to drive down there." After a pause, Tom looked at him intently. "You're in love with Melissa, aren't you?

As the realisation hit Nick, a light came on in his heart.

Of course I am. I love Lissy.

He was in love with her, but he also loved her. "I would feel as though my life was empty if..." He looked up at Tessa, who smiled.

"Exactly," she said. "It is up to you to convince her that it is a love worth fighting for."

"And now it's probably too late," Nick said desperately. "It's all my fault. She was probably upset with me and not concentrating on her driving."

Tom's car was parked out on the road and Tom directed Nick to the passenger seat and opened the back door for their mother. It was the longest trip of Nick's life. Traffic was light, but the winter fog had descended on the Ebor stretch of road and they had to slow to a crawl for about ten miles. Nick sat forward with his head in his hands, not saying a word, and Tessa reached over every so often and rubbed his shoulders.

"Have faith, son. She will be all right."

"She was able to send a text, mate, so she's conscious," Tom said.

"But it's been four hours and you haven't had another one. And the police haven't called," Nick said tersely before he slumped back into silence. Tom reminded him gently that there was no service on this part of the Great Dividing Range. As they approached the little village of Dorrigo, the fog cleared, and they were able to pick up their pace. Tom's phone beeped, and Nick grabbed it as Tom slowed down.

"Keep driving!" Nick yelled as he read the message. "It's from the police. All it says—*Car found. Please call*," and he read out the number for the police station.

"What does that mean? Where is she or have they found her and don't want to tell us by phone?" Nick's voice broke. "Why did I wait so long to tell her how I feel?"

Tessa undid her seat belt and reached over and put both arms around Nick.

"Mama, put your belt on. We don't want another injury tonight," Tom said quietly.
Tessa ignored him and spoke to Nick.

"Dominic, call the number and I will speak to them."

When they came over the edge of the escarpment and onto the road down the mountain, they saw the lights of the coastal towns twinkling in the distance.

"No good," groaned Nick. "Service has dropped out and it doesn't come back till we reach the valley along the river."

"Do you want to turn around and go back to pick up service?" asked Tom.

"No, just get down there." Nick's voice was harsh.

It was twenty minutes before they reached the bottom of the mountain road and came across a police officer in the middle of the road swinging a flashlight to slow them down.

Their headlights reflected off his yellow vest and he flagged them down with the bright light.

Tom pulled over to the side of the road and Nick was out of the car before it had stopped. He ran across to the policeman.

"Where is she? It's my—" he paused, "— my friend."

Tess and Tom came up behind him as the young constable answered. "We don't know. The car is wedged in a tree and there's nobody inside. There was no sign of any passengers. Do you know how many were in the car?"

"Just one," said Nick. He turned away fighting the nausea that clawed at his stomach. He heard Tom talking to the young police officer.

"What's happening?"

"They've sent to Bellingen for some big lights and a couple of officers have clambered down the bank. But so far there's no sign of anyone."

"Mate...brace yourself...they say there was a fair bit of blood in the car as well."

Tessa gave a small cry of distress and grabbed Nick's hand before leading him away from the middle of the road. It had started to rain again, but he was barely aware of the cold rain trickling past his collar.

"It's too late, Mama. I've lost her before I could even tell her how much I love her."

Another police car came slowly up the road towards them. Two officers got out of the car and had a short conversation with the constable who was slowing the traffic down. He pointed to Nick. They came over and explained that the search was not going to start until daylight.

"It's too dangerous in the dark, mate. You would be better off coming down to Bellingen and resting so you can join in at daylight." It took Tom and Tessa a long time to convince Nick that this was the best course of action. After giving the police their phone numbers and extracting a promise that they would be informed of any developments, they left. They drove to the Motor Inn at the east of town and booked one room. Tessa put the kettle on and Nick sat in the lounge. He was quiet, and Tom and Tessa spoke softly in the kitchenette as they made a cup of tea.

Tom opened the minibar fridge and pulled out a small bottle of brandy and tipped the lot into Nick's mug of tea.

"To help you get a bit of sleep, mate." Nick looked at him in disgust but drank the tea anyway.

Tessa curled up on the lounge next to Nick and held his hand. His fingers played with his mother's hand and he gradually relaxed a little.

Tom stretched out on the bed and they waited for a call.

##

Tom's phone rang as the dawn light began to pierce through the curtains. Nick grabbed for it and listened for a few seconds.

"We're on our way." He brushed his eyes impatiently. "They've found her, and she's just been taken to hospital to be checked over."

"Thank God!" cried Tessa.

"She walked to a farmhouse. I can't believe it. From where the car went over, she walked almost to town. She went knocking on a door as the dairy farmer was heading out to milk. She walked into the barn and the guy got a real shock."

Tom drove them the short distance into town and pulled up outside the little cottage hospital. Tom parked the car, while Nick and Tessa entered the office. There was no one to be seen and Nick paced impatiently.

"Calm down. It's only a little country hospital. The night nurses will be with Melissa and the doctor." Tess pushed him into the chair. As the automatic doors opened for Tom, a nurse came out of a room at the end of the corridor.

"Mr. Richards?" she asked.

"Yes," answered Tom and Nick together. She ushered them into the waiting room. "The doctor is with Ms. McIntyre now. Don't be too concerned. She's in pretty good shape. You can see her when the doctor has finished."

"Dr. McIntyre," corrected Nick. The nurse looked confused. "Oh, I didn't realise she was a doctor."

"A history doctor," said Nick proudly.

Chapter Twenty-One

The doctor finished checking Lissy over and the nurse stripped her wet clothes off and gave her a quick, warm shower before dressing her in a hospital gown.

"Now hop into bed and I'll bring you a hot cup of tea."

"I have to call my mother first; she'll be worried I didn't call her last night."

"It's okay," said the nurse. "Your fiancé is out in the waiting room. He can come in now that the doctor has given you the all clear. He wanted to do a precautionary head X-ray, but he's sure there's not a problem."

Lissy looked at her in total confusion. *She must be mistaken. There must be someone else in here with a fiancé waiting to see her.*

The nurse had grimaced as she washed Lissy's legs and pulled off a half dozen leeches. There were red marks down to her ankles where even more leeches had fallen off, sated with her blood. "A course of antibiotic to keep the bites from getting infected. All in all, young lady, you are very lucky."

She bustled out of the room and Lissy rolled over, burrowing her face into the soft pillow and closing her eyes. The door opened quietly a few minutes later.

"Just put it down there. I'm going to take a little nap before I drink it," she said in a sleepy voice. The nurse didn't answer, and she drifted off into a light doze, dreaming about what she had planned for Nick. She was standing outside his door, trying to knock, but someone kept holding her hand and wouldn't let it go. She murmured as she drifted in and out of a light doze, frustrated, but the warm grip on her hand got firmer.

Her eyes opened wide as she realised that someone was holding her hand tightly. Looking up, she saw Nick sitting in the chair close to the bed. Her eyes went down to her hand, which was locked in his.

"Good morning," he said softly.

"What are you doing here?" She shook her head slowly in disbelief.

"I'm here because I love you."

Her eyes filled with tears. She began to speak, and he put his fingers against her lips.

"Ssh. I want you to rest. The doctor says they will do an X-ray at eight a.m. when the staff arrives, and if it's clear, which he fully expects, I can take you home."

"Nick?" she asked before she drifted off again. "Would you please call Mum?"

"In Denmark?"

She giggled and went back to sleep.

***

Lissy was given the all clear as the doctor had expected and was discharged at lunchtime. Nick had sorted out the police reports and contacted the car rental company, and all Lissy had to do was sit in the back of Tom's car and enjoy the attention that Nick lavished on her during the two-hour trip. Tessa insisted that they all go back to the farm, and once there, she put Lissy to bed in the guest room. As Lissy sank into the feather soft mattress, she looked up at Tessa.

"I'm so happy. Pinch me and tell me I don't have a head injury." Tessa leaned down and kissed her cheek gently.

"You are not dreaming or concussed. However, you've made my dream come true. The first night I met you, I knew you were destined for this family. Even though it was not with my Tomas. I must go and rouse my husband from his study and tell him all is well." Tessa turned to leave the room and stood in the doorway, her beautiful face alight. "I'm so happy you're here, Lissy. I'm sure we will see you very often."

Tessa left and ushered Nick in, warning him

not to excite Lissy. "Even though she's fine, we need to let her rest."

"Mama, I'm not an insensitive boor."

"No, I think you left that at the door of the hospital, my Dominic." She reached over and kissed her son. "She is wonderful. Don't you let her go again."

Nick came in and sat on the side of the bed, looking down at her, happiness all over his face. He took her hand in one of his and smoothed her short curls with the other.

"I'm sorry, I got it cut off, Nick. I did it to upset you."

"I know," he said. "But I like it."

Lissy looked worried.

"It's okay," he said.

"No, it's not that," she said. He leaned forward.

"Are you in pain, should I call the doctor?"

"No, but we do have a problem. I've done something else."

He looked down at her, confusion on his face. "It's all right. After last night, when I thought I had lost you, nothing can be bad. What is it?"

"Well, I applied for a job, an associate professorship...and I got it." He looked so pleased for her, some of her worry lifted.

"That's wonderful."

"It is sort of. But...but it's in Auckland. New

Zealand."

Nick laughed. "I know where Auckland is."

His shoulders began to shake and Lissy sat up against the headboard of the bed.

"It's not funny. You'll be here, and I'll be across the Tasman Sea. I can't refuse it now."

"Oh, this is meant to be." Nick stopped laughing, but his lips were still upturned in a huge smile as he spoke. "That will be a great place for me to base myself to begin my next research project. I would much rather be out in the field, back on a boat than working from a university base. I can see myself living on a sailing boat in the marina in Auckland harbour. How would you feel about that?"

He leaned over and put his head on the pillow next to her. "You're still fragile," he said. "I don't know whether to ask you now."

Lissy looked up at him confused.

"Ask me what?"

"How would you feel about living on a boat in Auckland?"

Her answer was unspoken, and she demonstrated her acceptance to Nick's quiet satisfaction. She wound her arms around his neck and kissed him soundly, despite her fragility.

"I guess that's a yes," he said.

Lyn and Lars arrived when she woke from

her sleep and Lissy's happiness was complete. By early evening, the word had spread to the family and when Nick escorted her down to the living room, the room was overflowing with the noise of his family and all the children. Lissy looked over and was pleased to see Tom, standing with his arm around Jill, as Alex went over and punched his brother on the arm.

"Looking good for the life plan, Tomas."

"Alessandro. Manners!" Tessa chased her youngest son flicking her apron at him as they ran across the living room, with Alex screaming in mock horror.

She turned to Jill.

"I am sorry, Jill. My sons have no manners, they take after their father." Lissy and Nick looked at each other and burst out laughing. Tom joined in and leaned over to Jill.

"Don't worry, it is always a madhouse. Take me, take my family," She beamed up at him and Lissy whispered to Nick.

"A double wedding?"

"No way," said Nick. "We are going to have *our* special day and it won't be the typical Richards' madhouse." He pulled her close as though he would never let go.

Lissy leaned into him and closed her eyes. All was well with her world.

Epilogue

A light breeze carried the excited voices of children across the sand as the guests assembled on the beach. Three rows of chairs with white satin bows were placed in two semi-circles well back from the water's edge. Four men in formal suits looked decidedly out of place against the backdrop of the ocean and the rocks, peeking out in the low tide. A parade of well-dressed women and men took their seats and the marriage celebrant nodded at the young man who had a CD player mounted on a small table. He fiddled with the speaker and the haunting strains of "Even When I'm Sleeping" drifted across the assembled gathering.

Three ribbon-bedecked cars came slowly down the hill to the beach and the murmur of the group quietened as they stopped in the car park of Blackrock Beach. One of the young men waiting in the car park opened the door of the first bridal vehicle and put his hand out to assist the matron of honour from the car. Mrs Mac stepped out, resplendent in mauve lace and a large hat and gave a huge smile as she waved to those gathered on the beach. She turned and helped out the two little flower girls, one dressed in sky blue and the other in pink. The second car door opened, and Sophie, Ally and Lucy stepped out and the crowd sighed as they completed the colours of the rainbow with their bridal attire.

Necks craned as the door of the final vehicle opened and the females of the bridal party went over to assist the bride.

Lissy stepped from the vehicle and there was a collective ooh as the simple beauty of her wedding dress was displayed. Fresh flowers wound through her short curls and she carried a trailing bouquet of red rosebuds.

The volume of the music swelled as the group stepped on to the beach and an elderly gentleman put his hand out to lead Lissy to her groom.

Lissy smiled up at Harvey and felt the sheen of tears as she missed her Gramps for a fleeting moment. She closed her eyes and felt his presence in the gentle slough of the waves.

As Mrs Mac and the three sisters led her towards the waiting groom and his attendants, she smiled at the guests and as she passed the front row, Tessa and Lyn both reached out and kissed her gently. She smiled to see the tears of joy running down their faces and she looked up at Harvey, determined not to cry. She grinned as she saw the look on his face. She had never seen him clean shaven and hair trimmed before, but it was the look of pride on his face that made her smile. He looked as proud as any grandfather would.

They stepped towards the celebrant and Harvey placed her hand in Nick's. Sophie came over behind her and lifted her veil. Lissy looked up at Nick and was moved by the expression of sheer joy and love on his face.

He mouthed to her. "You are beautiful" as the strains of the music faded, and the ceremony began.

The gulls squawked overhead, and the waves pushed their way onto the sand edged with a froth like a bridal veil as Nick and Lissy made their promises to each other. A cheer went up as the celebrant pronounced them man and wife, and Nick pulled Lissy to him for a long and satisfying kiss.

A breeze light as a baby's breath and as warm as a kiss, teased curls from the flowers in her hair. Children let go of their parents' tight hands and ran down to paddle in the rock pools. Mrs Mac clutched her hat and held on to Harvey with her other hand as Tom looked down at Jill and she blushed when he kissed her lightly on the cheek. Tessa stood and looked at her brood with contentment and leaned over and squeezed her husband's arm.

"All is well with our family, yes?"

He smiled down at her. "*Sì, il mio amore.*"

Nick and Lissy were still in each other's arms.

He whispered against her mouth. "Forever, Lissy?"

"Forever, Nick," was the soft reply.

THE END

Book 2 Tom's story: Marry in Haste

Book 3 Alex's story: Outback Sunrise

Available on Annie's print bookstore with her other titles:
https://www.annieseaton.net/store.html

Visit Annie's website to subscribe to her newsletter to stay up to date with release dates: http://annieseaton.net

Other Books by Annie Seaton

Whitsunday Dawn

Undara

Osprey Reef

Porter Sisters Series

Kakadu Sunset

Daintree

Diamond Sky

Hidden Valley

Larapinta

Pentecost Island Series (2020)

Pippa

Eliza

Nell

Tamsin

Evie

Cherry

Odessa

Sienna

Tess

Isla

Pentecost Island 1-3

Pentecost Island 4-6

Pentecost Island 7-10

Bondi Beach Love Series

Beach House

ANNIE SEATON

Beach Music
Beach Walk
Beach Dreams
The House on the Hill Boxed Set

Prickle Creek Series
Her Outback Cowboy
Her Outback Surprise
His Outback Nanny
His Outback Temptation

Second Chance Bay Series
Her Outback Playboy
Her Outback Protector
Her Outback Haven
Her Outback Paradise

Love Across Time Series
Come Back to Me
Follow Me
Finding Home
The Threads that Bind

The Richards Brothers
The Trouble with Paradise
Marry in Haste
Crocodile Springs

Sunshine Coast
Waiting for Ana
The Trouble with Jack
Healing His Heart

Deadly Secrets
Adventures in Time
Silver Valley Witch
The Emerald Necklace
Ten Days in Tuscany
Worth the Wait
Full Circle
Baby It's Hot Outside

About the Author

Annie lives in Australia, on the beautiful north coast of New South Wales. She sits in her writing chair and looks out over the tranquil Pacific Ocean.

She writes contemporary romance and loves telling the stories that always have a happily ever after. She lives with her very own hero of many years and they share their home with Toby, the naughtiest dog in the universe, and Barney, the rag doll kitten, who hides when the four grandchildren come to visit.

If you would like to stay up to date with Annie's releases, subscribe to her newsletter here: http://www.annieseaton.net